Nick follo⋯⋯⋯⋯⋯⋯⋯⋯⋯⋯
time she ne⋯⋯

"I know t⋯⋯⋯⋯⋯⋯
into," he said. "And I'm sorry. I didn't mean
to do this to you."

She put her arms around his neck and pulled
him close. "I feel I can face any punishment,"
she said, "so long as I'm looking into your eyes.
Know this much, Nicholas Orton. No matter
what happens, I love you." She released him
and turned and moved away.

"Hold it right there," Monkey said behind
him.

Nick broke into a smile that felt as if it would
break his face wide open. "She said she still
loves me."

"Well, she's wrong," Monkey said.

"What?" Nick asked, staring at Monkey.

"By the gods, what a mess. You don't get it,
do you?"

"Get what?" Nick demanded. "She said she
loved me. And I love her. What is there to get?"

Monkey sho⋯⋯⋯ h⋯⋯ as if talking to a
child. "When ⋯⋯⋯⋯⋯⋯⋯⋯⋯⋯⋯ she
loses her powe⋯⋯⋯⋯⋯⋯⋯⋯⋯⋯ ready
starting to ha⋯⋯⋯⋯⋯⋯⋯⋯⋯⋯ anymore."

Nick looked ⋯⋯⋯⋯⋯⋯⋯⋯⋯ stand.
How can I change—"

"Break her heart," Monkey said.

Hallmark Entertainment Books

JOURNEY TO THE CENTER OF THE EARTH
Jules Verne

LEPRECHAUNS
Craig Shaw-Gardner

THE 10th KINGDOM
Kathryn Wesley

ARABIAN NIGHTS
Kathryn Wesley

THE MONKEY KING

Kathryn Wesley

based on a teleplay by
David Henry Hwang

HALLMARK ENTERTAINMENT BOOKS

HALLMARK ENTERTAINMENT BOOKS are published by

Kensington Publishing Corp.
850 Third Avenue
New York, NY 10022

First Hallmark Entertainment Books Paperback Printing: January, 2001

10 9 8 7 6 5 4 3 2 1

Printed in the United States of America

For Bill Trojan
Thanks for all the help.

An Introduction to *The Monkey King*

Dear Reader,

Once upon a time, Nicholas Orton was a Chinese scholar. But lost love damaged his heart and made him turn his back on his passion. So, at the beginning of *The Monkey King*, Nick is bringing business to China—cold, heartless business. Along the way, he gets enticed by a woman who resembles the goddess Kwan Ying in *The Monkey King* paintings. Nick is charmed and enchanted by all he sees in China, but nothing charms him more than Kwan Ying.

She persuades him to go on a magical quest to find the original lost manuscript for *Journey to the West*. And here is where our story collides with history. The book *Journey to the West* actually exists. It's based on the true story of a famous Chinese monk, Xuan Zang. Xuan Zang traveled on foot to what we now know as India to see the Sutra, the Buddhist holy book. When he returned to China, he translated the Sutra into Chinese, which helped Buddhism flourish in China.

Journey to the West is one of the great allegorical journeys in world literature. It fictionalizes Xuan Zang's real life adventure by mixing that story with Chinese fables, fairy tales, legends and superstitions. The Monkey King features prominently in the story. In fact, most English texts have renamed the book, calling it *Monkey* instead. It's a comic novel, attributed to Wu Cheng'en, and in it, you will find familiar characters, from Monkey himself to Pigsy to Xuan Zang.

Our mini-series follows the structure of *Journey to the West,* using many of its tropes, to create a story set in modern times. In some ways, Nick's journey parallels that of Xuan Zang, an outsider searching for a book that will change the world. *Journey to the West* is more than a book, and it changes everything in Nick's life, from his beliefs about life to his beliefs about himself. His adventure opens his heart and allows him to love again, although the person he falls in love with happens to be an actual goddess, one who will lose her powers if she lets her emotions overtake her.

Then, of course, there is the Monkey King himself. The central figure in *Journey to the West,* Monkey is rescued from beneath a mountain in *The Monkey King* to help Nick with this new journey. Along the way, Monkey (who is both a comic and dangerous character) discovers strengths he never knew he had.

If you love *The Monkey King,* and want to continue your reading experience, you'll find a number of copies of *Journey to the West* in translation including one, called *Monkey,* that many universities use as the definitive text. You can also find theatrical productions, ballets, comic books and a Japanese TV show, all about the Monkey King. And if you go to Guangzhou (Canton) Guangdong Province in China, you will find a gigantic walk-through attraction (what we in the States would call a theme park) centered on the Monkey King.

Of course, you won't find Nicholas in any of

these works. But fiction and history are not so easily separated. If you continue your own quest after watching *The Monkey King*, you will discover Nicholas's passion, much as he rediscovers it. You'll see what drew him to Chinese scholarship, and ultimately to Kwan Ying.

Stories can do many things. Just like they do in *The Monkey King*, stories can make us rethink our priorities and sometimes they enable us to change the world.

Sincerely,

Robert Halmi, Sr.
Chairman, Hallmark Entertainment, Inc.
Executive Producer, *The Monkey King*

One

"They look almost alive," the only woman in the small group of tourists said, her voice hushed, awe clear in every word.

Her words were swallowed up by the vast underground chamber filled with a mighty army of soldiers, all frozen in stone—thousands of them, different yet the same, standing in perfect lines, on guard for all time. The chamber seemed to go on forever, over and around the stone men, covering them from the ravages of the weather.

Each statue was clothed in the traditional dress of a Chinese warrior of two thousand years before. Each held his weapon with clear pride and knowledge.

"The famous Terracotta Warriors," Nicholas Orton told the four people with him, barely keeping the awe out of his own voice. He took a deep breath of the dry, dirt-smelling air, and stared at the rows and rows of soldiers. For years he had seen only pictures of this sight. But he had studied every detail, even how to tell the ranks of uniforms apart.

As a child, he'd sworn that someday he would walk among the Terracotta Warriors, talk to them as if they were his friends, study them for every detail he could learn about their history.

Now he was here. It was hard to believe. Only it wasn't to study, but as a tour guide.

With the rest of the group he was leading, he stood and just stared in silence. He had always understood that they looked almost alive. That had not been a myth. They did, but he had not expected they would also look very dangerous.

Industrialist Marcus Harding moved silently up beside Nick. Nick was the tour guide for Harding and his group, even though Nick had never been to most of the places they were touring. But he knew of them, knew about them, better than most. He had gotten both a bachelor and masters degree in Chinese history and myth in Chicago. Ten years ago, he had quit his study for his doctorate in the same area to try to get some of the money big business offered.

Now, thanks to that decision, he found himself in a place he had always wanted to visit, the Shaanxi Provincial Museum. This was a long, long way from his home town in the Midwest, that was for sure. A long way from those college days of studying this place.

He'd known from the moment he stepped into this massive chamber that he could come to love this ongoing archaeological dig, and the way this massive chamber stayed cold even on the hottest days. This was one of very few tombs open to the public. Given time, he might get into extra tombs that had been opened, maybe see things only archaeologists had seen.

His passion since he was a boy had been anything Chinese, and now he was standing in one of the most inspiring places from Chinese history.

He glanced around at the group, then around the chamber. Only his people were in here at the moment, yet he couldn't shake the feeling he was being watched. More than likely he was. In China, anything was possible.

Elizabeth, a tall, attractive blond who had been hitting on him since he had first met Harding's party at the airport, moved up beside him, staring at the soldiers spread out before them in perfect rows.

"So lifelike," she said. "It's almost spooky."

Nick agreed completely. "Each one was modeled after some real person more than two thousand years ago."

"How many are there?" Elizabeth asked, moving even closer to him.

"About seven thousand." Nick eased away like an animal from the gaze of a predator.

Benjamin, who seemed more like a computer whiz kid than someone who belonged in the high-stakes world of business, whistled softly at the number.

"So this Emperor," Benjamin asked, "he really went out in style, huh?"

"Let's just say he didn't like to go anywhere without his army," Nick said, glancing at Elizabeth, then moving away to turn to face the entire group. "The Emperor Qin Shi Huangdi spent his whole life building massive under-ground tombs around here. One of them is even supposed to contain a replica of all China."

"I'd like to see that," Benjamin said.

Clark, the silent Englishman, nodded.

"The tomb has never been opened." Nick smiled at Benjamin, then glanced at Harding.

"Why not?" Elizabeth asked. "Wouldn't it be the ultimate tourist attraction?"

"How about it, Mr. Harding?" Benjamin asked. "Think there's an investment opportunity here?"

Harding only grunted and glanced at Nick with those cold, dark eyes Nick didn't really trust. If Harding hadn't been paying him so much money, he'd never have worked for him. But sometimes business required working for people he didn't like, as Nick had quickly found out a number of years back.

"I'm afraid I'd have to advise against that," Nick said. "You see, the tomb entrance is sup-posed to be littered with booby traps. Emperor Huangdi made sure that the price of admission into his prize chamber would be death."

"Thanks, Nick." Harding shook his head in amusement. "Good safety tip."

Nick was about to go into some of his knowl-edge about the Terracotta Warriors when his cell phone beeped in his jacket pocket. He glanced down at it, surprised it would even work in this cavern.

"Sorry," Nick said, glancing at Harding as he

stepped away. When he was five paces back he put the phone to his ear. "Yeah?"

"Mr. Orton," a woman's voice said in perfect English, "General Wang would like to talk to you about a job for his cousin."

"Who?" Nick's voice filled the chamber. Suddenly he realized General Wang would be one of the main ministers approving Harding's project. "Christ, just patch me through directly."

He turned to the group. "Please, go on ahead into the next chamber. Just stay on the path and don't touch anything."

Harding glanced at him questioningly, but Nick motioned everything would be all right.

"They seem like they might kill you at any moment," Benjamin said to Elizabeth as he fell in beside her.

"Yeah," Elizabeth said. "I'm almost afraid to turn my back on them."

At the moment Nick was less concerned about turning his back on stone statues than about making this phone call work for him and Harding. He walked ten paces away from the edge of the warriors and stopped, listening carefully.

"General Wang," Nick said as the phone clicked into life, "it's always such a pleasure to hear from you."

Behind Nick one of the stone warriors blinked, looked up at Nick's back, then at the warrior beside it. It made no rock-scraping-on-rock sound; its movements were those of a flesh-and-blood soldier.

"Psssst," the terracotta warrior said to the one on his right. "That's him."

The warrior next to the first came to life and looked around at Nick. "Took him long enough to get here."

A third warrior, this one behind the first, shook his head as a number of the stone statues turned to look at Nick Orton's back. "It's too late. This world is doomed. Too bad, too."

Suddenly, without a sound, as Nick continued to talk, a woman wearing exquisite Tang dynasty silk and a beautiful headdress appeared out of nowhere. She floated on a cloud just in front of the warriors. Her beauty was almost too much to look at directly. Her features were fine and perfectly formed, her eyes full of life. An unseen breeze blew the silk around her legs and waist.

As one, thousands of stone warriors bowed.

"Kwan Ying," the first warrior said. "The Goddess of Mercy. You have come."

Kwan Ying said nothing, but instead turned and stared at Nick's back as he continued to talk.

Many of the warriors followed her gaze.

"Goddess," a second warrior asked, "is there still time for the scholar to fulfill his destiny?"

She glanced out at the mass of stone soldiers, now all very much alive. They turned and stared at her intently, waiting for the answer.

"I believe there is still time, but I must find

a way to gain his trust," Kwan Ying said. "He is our only hope."

"You, oh great goddess, can do it," one warrior said.

Others joined in, agreeing.

She held up her hands for silence from the mass of stone figures.

"I have no other choice."

They all nodded, agreeing. She had no other choice if the world was to be saved.

Then, as Nick clicked his cell phone shut and the Terracotta Warriors became silent and still once again, she faded away, leaving only a faint breeze to disturb Nick's hair.

TWO

Nick followed his group from the dig and into the first few rooms of the Shaanxi Provincial Museum, giving details when asked, but mostly just allowing himself to enjoy his first visit as well. He wished he was here to work on his own research, but that would come with time, he was sure. Right now he was working at making money, and that had gotten him here sooner than he ever would have expected as a researcher.

The phone call had turned out to be a positive one. Nick had gotten some concessions from the general for more freedom for Harding and his company in exchange for some basic job considerations later for members of the General's family. Harding had been pleased when Nick had pulled him aside and told him.

Right now Harding and Benjamin were talking about something they clearly didn't want anyone else to hear. Clark, the Englishman, followed Elizabeth, who followed Nick.

"And what is that?" Elizabeth asked, pointing to a series of late eighteenth-century panels.

Nick knew exactly what those panels were and

what story they portrayed, but at the moment he had no desire to talk about them. They were part of the area in which he had done his most basic study while in school.

"He's a famous Chinese god," Nick said, "the Monkey King." He turned and pointed to another exhibit just ahead. "Over here, there're some amazing Tang dynasty silks."

For the first time, Elizabeth didn't follow him.

"Why is he trapped underneath that rock?" She pointed to a scene on one panel.

Harding and Benjamin moved over and stared at the panels, leaving Nick standing alone a short distance ahead. It seemed he had no choice. He sighed and moved back to stand near the first panel.

"Does he ever get out?" she asked.

"He's trapped under a mountain," Nick said. "Not a rock. And according to the legend, the Goddess of Mercy, Kwan Ying, comes down from heaven and tells Monkey"—Nick pointed to the figure who had his lower half under the miniature mountain—"that a priest will pass this way on a pilgrimage to India to fetch the sacred scriptures of Buddha."

"Wow," Elizabeth said.

Harding only snorted.

"The priest frees Monkey," Nick continued, "to serve as the holy man's protector and disciple."

Nick moved on down the line of panels, relaying the rest of the story.

"Together with a giant pig named Pigsy and a monster named Friar Sand, they manage to bring the sacred scrolls, through a series of adventures, back to China." Nick pointed to the last panel.

"How do you know all this stuff?" Benjamin stared at Nick as if he were an alien from another planet.

Nick remembered the first time he had ever read the legend and seen pictures of the panels. He couldn't have been more than ten, yet it had become one of the most important stories in his life. Of course, he wasn't about to tell Harding and his little group that.

"Back in college," Nick said, "I was going to write my dissertation on *Journey to the West*. That's the novel about the Monkey King's adventures."

"There's a novel?" Elizabeth asked. "Not just the panels?"

"There is," Nick said. "You can buy wonderful editions of it just about anywhere."

His phone rang again.

"Excuse me." Nick stepped away and put the phone to his ear. "Yes?"

"Hello, Mr. Orton," a woman's voice said. The tone was soft and very clear. "I am the secretary for Minister Kwan."

"Who?" Nick asked.

"Minister Kwan from the Ministry of Public Works," the woman said. "She would like to meet with you as soon as possible."

Nick's throat closed up slightly at the mention of the Ministry of Public Works. Harding had a very important bid coming up there tomorrow—the very bid that would keep Nick on staff with Harding if it worked. If the bid was accepted, Harding and his company would be the main contractors on a massive new business complex to be built near this very museum. No doubt this Kwan wanted a little something extra from her vote on the bid, just as the General had done. Such were the ways of China. Harding had already paid more outright bribes than Nick ever could have imagined.

"I've never heard that name before," Nick said, trying to keep his voice friendly, "but I will gladly meet with the minister." He glanced at the group down the corridor. "I can meet in front of my hotel, the Sheraton, in one hour."

"Fine," the woman said.

The phone went dead, as if it had never been connected.

Nick clicked it shut and moved back to the group.

"Anything I should know, Nick?" Harding asked as Nick returned to his position in front of the group.

"Mr. Harding, you hired me to help you get the contract," Nick said, "not to bother you with every detail."

"I'm old fashioned." Harding's dark eyes bored through Nick.

For some reason, Nick didn't want to tell Harding about this meeting. There was little doubt it would be just like many others he had suffered through, but it seemed Harding wanted to know everything and was giving Nick no choice.

"Same old water torture," Nick said. "Some

bureaucrat summoning me for yet another urgent meeting."

"Does this have something to do with us?" Harding asked.

"Maybe." Nick shrugged. "Maybe not. This official works for the Ministry of Public Works. The same office that's going to hear your bid tomorrow." He smiled.

"Like to cover all your bases, do you?" Harding asked.

"Don't you, sir?" Nick asked. "Besides, it's my job to make sure you enter China the right way: through the back door and with the bid in your pocket completely approved. So if you'll excuse me . . ."

Nick glanced at his watch, but it took him a moment to realize something was wrong. The time wasn't right, and the little hand was swirling backward.

"Something wrong?" Harding asked.

"No." Nick tapped his watch. "It's strange. I just bought this a month ago."

As he watched, the little hand slowed and stopped, then started forward again as normal. For some reason, it gave him the chills. Something nudged his memory and then was gone.

"Swiss precision not what it used to be?" Harding asked.

"Evidently not." Nick laughed. He pointed down the corridor. "I have to head for the hotel for this meeting. The rest of the museum is pretty much self-explanatory. Have fun."

"It would be more fun if you were along," Elizabeth said.

Harding snorted. Nick walked out, glad to be away from her.

The heat on the street in front of the hotel was like being in a sauna. Nick could almost see the waves coming up off the pavement. Why he had told this diplomat to meet him in front of the hotel instead of inside, in the comfort of the air conditioning, was beyond him. Sometimes he was just too stupid for words.

The sun was low enough in the evening sky to keep almost everything in shade, but that just seemed to make the air stickier. His shirt was clinging to his back, and sweat plastered his hair to the side of his head.

He paced along the front wall of the hotel, watching the cars pulling up and the people crowding the streets. Of course this stupid diplomat would be late. It couldn't be any other way with him waiting out here.

"Scholar!" a voice behind Nick said.

Nick glanced around, but saw no one near enough to have spoken to him. And no one had ever called him *Scholar* anyway.

"Hey, you with the dumb look on your face. I'm talking to you."

Nick glanced up at a poster advertising the Monkey King exhibition at the museum. The reproduction featured the panel in which Monkey, a half-man, half-monkey creature, was trapped under the mountain.

Monkey was staring out of the poster at him. Not at all like the panel. Weird. Why would someone change a panel like that for advertising?

"We need you *now,*" Monkey said from the poster, "before it's too late."

Nick was sure he saw the figure in the poster move. He laughed and wiped his forehead. The heat was getting to him. He was seeing posters talking to him. He moved away from the poster and leaned against one wall of the hotel.

"Everythin' all right, Mr. Orton?" the doorman asked in English that had a little Bronx accent.

"Fine." Nick shook his head and looked back at the poster, which was now as it should be, with Monkey under the mountain. "Just working a little too hard is all."

"Well, if ya need anythin'," the doorman said.

"Thanks," Nick said.

Across the street, a Chinese woman in a striking black dress with a plunging neckline seemed to be looking around for someone. She had on dark glasses and carried no purse. Without even glancing at the traffic, she stepped into the street to cross toward Nick. For an instant, Nick didn't realize what was happening. There was no traffic on her side of the road.

But there was a very large truck on his side, moving fast, as trucks often did in this city when even the slightest stretch of road was open ahead of them.

Surely she would see it coming and stop on the center divider.

But her attention seemed to be focused on

the people, the buildings, even the sky. Every-thing *but* the oncoming truck.

"Stop!" Nick shouted at her, stepping to the edge of the sidewalk and motioning for her to remain on the center strip in the road.

She didn't seem to hear him. She reached the center strip and just kept coming, her smile focused on him as though she had known him for years.

As she stepped down into the street, the truck honked and hit its brakes. There was no chance it was going to stop if she didn't move and move quickly.

She looked at it, frozen in the moment.

In ten running steps, he had her by the shoulders. He let his momentum and grip carry them both back onto the median strip as the truck slid past them, its tires screaming on the pavement, its front bumper barely missing Nick's heel.

Under his fingers, her skin felt divine, as if made of satin. The force of his grab had knocked her sunglasses off. Her deep brown eyes were full of shock, as if the world had al-most ended at that moment.

"Are you all right?" he asked, making sure she was steady on her feet.

"Yes," the woman said in a voice that seemed to surround Nick and block out everything else. "Thank you. I guess I'm not used to traffic. For-give me, that was foolish."

The truck driver, with a few well-chosen words, sped away.

Nick let go of her, missing the feel of her skin

almost at once. He quickly picked up her sunglasses and handed them to her.

"It can happen to anyone," Nick said. "That's why our mothers always told us to look both ways before crossing the street."

He mentally kicked himself. Could he have thought of anything more stupid to say at that moment? Not likely.

"Did they?" she asked, then nodded. "That's good advice. I shall remember it."

He looked into her eyes and didn't have the slightest idea if she was playing with him or not. And honestly, she was so beautiful he didn't care. She could play all she wanted. He was instantly smitten. He had never seen skin so smooth, eyes so full, and a body so perfect for the low-cut black dress she was wearing.

"You sure you are all right?" he asked one more time, hoping to continue any kind of conversation with her.

"Yes, thank you," she said. She touched his cheek and looked at him as if he were a god. "You risked your life for me. I will always be in your debt."

His heart leaped and he swore, for just a moment, he heard the Hallelujah Chorus in the background. He couldn't believe how genuine her words sounded. Something about her voice seemed to control him—and with a woman as beautiful as she was, he wanted to be controlled.

"Look," Nick said, glancing around as cars sped past on both sides of them, "we've got to at least get out of the middle of the road. Why don't you come into the hotel? I'll buy you a drink. You can catch your breath."

"Well, actually—"

He interrupted her, not wanting her to say no. "I'm supposed to be meeting some obnoxious bureaucrat who is late—as usual."

"Mr. Orton?" she asked, smiling at him.

"You know my name?" Nick asked, shocked, his heart now stopped cold. How could she have known his name unless . . .

"I'm your late appointment." She smiled at him, a twinkle in her eyes. "The obnoxious bureaucrat."

The heat of the late afternoon again smashed down on him as he tried to catch his breath. Every inch of his body broke into a sweat. This was one meeting that wasn't going at all the way he had planned. Maybe *he* should just step in front of a truck and get this embarrassment over with.

"Oh, right," he managed to say as she looked up at him. "How red is my face? I'm sorry, but I—"

She laughed, high and fine, like a wonderful bell filling the air with music. "You can insult me all night, and I will still be eternally grateful."

"I have no intention of ever insulting you again." He smiled, very glad she was letting him take his foot out of his mouth.

"Come," she said. "I will buy *you* a drink."

"Good idea," he replied. "I think I'm going to need it."

Again she laughed. As far as Nick was concerned, that laugh could stop every speeding truck in all of China.

It almost stopped his heart.

"So what would you like?" he asked as he steered her to a seat at the bar. Around them the room was packed, every table full of patrons from all over the world, yet he felt as if they were the only two in the place.

She sat on the stool as if she had never done anything like it before. Her hands felt the wood of the bar rail, and her gaze took in the crowd that filled the tables.

"I don't know." She seemed puzzled as she stared at all the bottles. "What will you drink?"

"Something to take the taste of shoe leather out of my mouth," he said, but she didn't change expression, clearly missing his joke. "Better make it a dry martini."

"Very well," she said as the bartender placed two napkins in front of them. "Two martinis, please. Not very wet?"

Nick laughed and she smiled back. Right then he knew he could spend a lifetime looking into her eyes and never really understand how deep they were. There was something about this woman that was very, very special.

"Would you believe me if I told you now that I enjoy meeting officials from the Ministry?"

"No." She laughed in that faint, bell-like way that seemed to drive out all other noise. "But I do believe now that you are a good and honest man."

He felt instant embarrassment at her compliment, as if he knew deep down he was not worthy of it. She sure knew how to get to him, to punch every one of his buttons.

"Well, don't tell anyone," Nick said, managing to laugh. "It'll ruin my reputation as a ruthless capitalist."

"Not a word," she said.

He stared at her for a moment, then caught himself and went on, forcing himself to the business at hand, even though it was the last thing he really wanted to talk about. "So how can I help you? Someone looking for a job with Mr. Harding, or do you need to raise some money?"

"Not exactly." She shook her head slowly, clearly worried about what she was about to ask him.

"Well then," he said, hoping to ease her into it, "what can I do to help you? Anything. Just name it."

She glanced around as if to make sure no one could hear them. In this crowd, even sitting side-by-side at the bar, he was lucky to hear her. "Mr. Orton, this will strike you as extremely unorthodox . . ."

At that moment the bartender stepped up and placed the two martinis on the napkins, stopping her in midsentence.

Nick waited for him to leave, then reached forward and picked up a glass, removing the olive.

She did the same, staring at the clear liquid as if she had never seen anything like it before.

"To new friends," he said.

He reached over and clinked his glass lightly against hers.

She seemed puzzled by that motion as well.

Then he took a drink, relishing the taste he had learned to love back in college, indicating she should do the same.

She took much more than a sip. She downed the entire martini in one swig, grimacing at the taste.

He managed not to laugh. "When was the last time you had an alcoholic drink?"

"Oh," she said, staring at the empty glass in her hand, "it's been thousands of years."

He was about to ask her what she meant by years when she hiccupped.

"Excuse me," she said, staring into his eyes. "I mean thousands of days."

"Whatever." Nick was again lost in her gaze, as if the moment would go on for ever and ever.

Maybe it did. He had no idea and didn't care, as long as he was gazing into those eyes.

She broke the look and set her glass down. He finished his drink, glanced around, and caught the bartender's attention, indicating they wanted two more drinks.

Quickly.

This was turning out to be a very, very interesting meeting—one he hoped he was going to remember for a very long time.

Three

Nick watched as the woman who called herself Minister Kwan got quickly sloshed. In all his life he had never seen such an easy drunk, nor as beautiful a one. He had managed to convince her to sip her second martini, but by the time she had finished it, she was clearly feeling no pain.

Even better, she was laughing at his jokes and stories. He had just finished telling her about the time he had met the governor of the local province. The governor had talked about Nick in Chinese, right in front of him, unaware Nick understood every word.

She found the story far, far funnier than it should have been, then reached for her empty glass.

Nick put his hand on hers, enjoying the feel of her skin. "I think you've had enough."

"Even though I sipped the second one?" she asked, staring at him like a child asking for a bottle. He loved those eyes, that laugh. And he wanted to get to know them better, as well as the rest of her.

He was finding her even more irresistible

than before. If they were going to get their business done, it would have to be soon. Or not tonight at all.

"Listen," Nick said, "you still haven't told me why you wanted to see me."

She took and deep breath and nodded. "Yes, thank you for reminding me of my duty."

She glanced around, then lowered her voice. "Your world is in terrible danger. You are the only person who can save it."

Nick stared at her for a long moment, trying to wait until she broke out laughing again. But she seemed serious, or at least had the best poker face of anyone he had ever seen, especially drunk.

"Tell you what," Nick said, "let's go outside and get some fresh air."

"Good idea." She picked up her glass and ran her tongue around the rim.

Nick took her arm and eased her off the bar stool. Her legs were wobbly and she laughed at every step, but somehow he got her moving. After a short and thankfully uneventful walk across the lobby, they emerged into the warm early evening air of the city. The streets were still busy, but the buildings were shrouded in shadows and the temperature had dropped a little. The outdoor market was close by, and Nick steered them in that direction.

"Look at all this," she said, her arm sweeping around to include the market, the city, and the street. "Life in your world is so wonderful."

Nick glanced down at her, but she didn't notice. She was much more interested in staring at everything around them, as if she were seeing it for the first time.

"You keep saying *my* world," Nick said. "I thought this was your country."

"But it is *your* world."

He didn't ask anything more. Before he got a straight answer out of her, he was going to have to let the drinks wear off.

They walked, her arm firmly holding his as she stared at everything like a child.

Finally, just as Nick was going to suggest they turn around and head back toward the hotel, she stopped at a book stall and picked up a book. Nick glanced at it, then shook his head. Clearly he was having a day that kept reminding him what he had left behind in college. The book was a beautifully illustrated volume with the Monkey King on the cover.

"Journey to the West," she said, as if in awe at the very words. "This edition is exquisite."

"That it is," Nick said. "You know, I saw the Monkey King exhibit today. Afterward, right before meeting you, I had the experience of the image of the Monkey King trying to talk to me—from a poster, if you can believe that."

He expected her to laugh, but she didn't. And she was becoming sober very quickly. She *should* have laughed.

"You know"—she turned the book over in her hands—"that the original manuscript has been lost for centuries."

"I know," Nick said. "Actually, while studying in college, I came up with the theory that the manuscript was hidden in one of the unopened tombs right around here. I even thought I had figured out a way to get past the booby traps."

"You were a China scholar?" she asked, not so much out of surprise, but as if she were checking.

"It seems like a long time ago," Nick said, nodding. "I was close to finishing my doctorate when I woke one morning and realized that tenure was going to earn me a grand total of forty-five thousand dollars per year, and that wasn't even enough to get here, to the place I was studying so hard." Nick looked into her deep eyes and then shrugged. "So I sold out, got a degree in business, and here I am."

She took him by the arm and turned him toward a nearby park. "Actually, that is exactly what I need to speak with you about."

He laughed. "The ministry wants to discuss my lost dreams and unfinished degree?"

It was her turn to laugh, not with the force brought on by the drinks, but in the natural, bell-like way that he was learning to love very quickly.

Around them in the park, couples were walking and sitting on benches, talking and necking. He felt as if they belonged here. The warm air now was a comfortable blanket that surrounded them. Nick stopped and looked her directly in the eye.

"I've got to tell you," he said, "that I've never had this much fun before with a government official."

She laughed. "I'll bet you say that to all the bureaucrats."

"Never," he said. "And to tell you the truth, never to anyone else before, either."

They were staring at each other, and Nick felt like he needed to bend down and kiss this woman. He hadn't felt such an instant attraction to anyone in a long, long time. Never anything this quick and intense.

"To tell you the truth," she said, her voice soft and very alluring, "it's been a very long time since anyone has taken care of me the way you have tonight."

Nick laughed, remembering her weird comment earlier. "How long? Thousands of years?"

"Yes," she said, a look of complete sincerity filling her face. "Thousands of years."

He had nothing at all to say to that. He had been joking, but it seemed she believed what she was saying. Why couldn't he be attracted to a simple, sane woman?

Her wonderful eyes had just about convinced him it didn't matter if she were sane or not, he was going to kiss her, when suddenly people in the park around them started shouting and pointing.

They both glanced in the direction the others were indicating. In the evening light, Nick could see a radio station tower on a hill overlooking the city. But as he watched, the tower slowly became transparent.

Then it came back to solid again.

"Weird," he said. "Nifty trick."

"Dear Buddha," she said, "it's already starting to happen."

"What?" Nick looked at her, then back up at

the tower as once again it faded out, then returned. "What's happening?"

"The clock is turning back," she said.

The image of his watch running backward earlier flashed into his mind. "What are you talking about?"

She turned and pulled him back toward the market and the book stall, not saying another word. There she picked up the Monkey King volume and opened it.

"See," she said, pointing at the pages, "the book is starting to disappear from your world."

Nick could not believe his eyes. As she flipped through the pages, the words were fading away.

Around them a few people screamed.

Nick glanced up just in time to see the radio tower completely vanish.

"Do you know what's going on?" He turned her so he could see her every expression.

"There's no more time to explain," she said. "I can take you immediately where you need to go. But this will work only if you trust me."

He looked into her dark eyes and he knew, without a doubt, that he trusted her. He didn't know why, but he did.

"All right," he said.

She took his hand as the crowds around them moved at a frantic pace. She closed her eyes and tipped her head back, holding his hand firmly.

"I trust you."

As he said the words, a cloud appeared under them.

Nick could feel himself being lifted from the ground.

Then the world as he knew it vanished.

And so did her grip on his hand.

Four

It was as if someone had flicked off the lights for a moment, then snapped them back on. Only Nick wasn't in the same place when the lights came on as when they had been shut off. The city sounds and crowded streets, the shouting and the panic, were gone, as if he had only dreamed them. He was alone, facing a dirt wall, in very faint light.

His breath caught in his throat, and his heart pounded as he fought to control his fear. The air around him was dry and cool, which made him sweat even more.

He reached out a hand and touched the cold earth, letting the reality of the feeling calm him a little.

"OK, that's dirt," he whispered. He glanced around, trying to force his eyes to adjust to the dim light. There was no sign of the woman who had asked him to trust her.

"Hello!" His shout echoed and then died off. He was clearly in a big room, but he still couldn't see anything except the nearby wall and vague shapes. "Where am I?"

No answer.

He stepped away from the wall toward some
shadows, then realized he had come face to face
with the Terracotta Warriors. Suddenly he knew
exactly where he was.

Everything snapped into place and his panic
eased back slightly. He had been transported,
somehow, back to the archaeological dig.

Or maybe he had never left this afternoon.
Maybe the entire time with the woman had
been a dream. That seemed much more likely.
Harding probably was standing in the other
room with the rest, wondering what had happened to him.

Suddenly, from a side corridor that led away
from the path to the museum, a familiar voice
said, "Please, follow me. Quickly."

Nick caught a glimpse of her as she turned
and moved away into the dirt-walled corridor.

So she had been real. Either that or he was
still dreaming.

He ran after her. "Wait. How did I get here?
What have you done to me?" He needed some
answers, and he needed them fast. At the moment, she was the only one who could give
them to him.

The corridor was long and slanted downward
slightly. There was no place for her to have left
the corridor, so he kept running. She had to
be ahead of him somewhere. After a few hundred steps he started wondering why the archaeologists had even dug this tunnel. It felt as
if it were headed in the direction of where some
of the other tombs were supposed to be.

He forced himself to calm down. If this was a dream, he'd wake up soon enough.

Finally, the corridor dead-ended into a dirt wall. She stood there, clearly waiting for him.

"All right." Nick fought to catch his breath as he stopped in front of her. "Let me see if I got this right. You are not really from the Ministry of Public Works, are you?"

"Forgive me," she said. "It was the only way I knew to enlist your help."

"My help for *what?*" Nick almost shouted the last word. His frustration with all this was right on the surface.

Without giving him an answer, she touched his face lightly, then said, "Trust me."

Then she put her hands together, turned to the wall, and started chanting. "Om mani padme hum."

"What are you doing?"

"Om mani padme hum . . . om mani padme hum . . ."

Around them the ground started to rumble. Nick put his hand against the shaking dirt wall and looked up at the roof. There were no supports. A good earthquake would bury them alive. "Oh, shit . . ."

He glanced back up the long dirt tunnel. "We've got to get out of here and fast, or we are going to be breathing dirt!"

She didn't move.

The ground shook even harder, rocking Nick against the wall as he started to grab her and try to make a run for it.

Dust rained down on them as slowly a light appeared from a crack in the dead-end wall.

Nick braced himself and stared, dumbfounded.

She didn't seem to notice the danger they were in, or the light. Instead she stood, calmly chanting, hands together, facing the wall of new light. This was one very strange woman he had fallen for.

Finally the crack in the wall irised completely open with a *shuck* sound, forming some sort of gateway which seemed to shimmer like a rainbow painted on the surface of glowing water.

Around them, the shaking stopped and the dust settled.

"This can't be happening." Nick stared at the shimmering light and knew for certain he was dreaming.

She turned to him and made him look into her eyes. There he could see she was pleading with him to continue. Fine. But Nick still couldn't believe any of this was real.

Suddenly, a flash of light changed her from a woman dressed in a wonderful low-cut gown to an even more beautiful woman wearing Tang dynasty silks and a goddess headdress. On top of that, she had the longest fingernails he had ever seen.

Nick staggered back from her, stopping only when he banged into the dirt wall. She was clearly the same woman he had met in front of the hotel, which meant his dream was getting even weirder.

"Do you know what this is?" She indicated the swirling, color-filled end of the tunnel.

He remembered his myths well. "An entrance to one of the unexcavated tombs," he answered. "The writings say that a person wanting entrance must enter the world by stepping through a wall of shimmering light, if I remember right."

He could see from her smile that she agreed.

"But you don't want to go in there," he warned. "The entrances are all rigged with booby traps."

"Follow me," she said, her voice even more beautiful and comforting than it had been in the hotel.

Damn. He was a sucker for a good-looking woman, even one with long fingernails. She was almost making him want to go through that light.

She turned and stepped through the opening, disappearing as if submerged. The last thing he saw of her was her shoulder and right foot.

"No!" Nick shouted, jumping to grab her. "You'll be killed!"

Way too late. She was gone.

He stopped at the edge of the aurora-like surface. It swirled in reds and blues and greens, so fast he couldn't see his reflection, let alone where she had gone.

"You are going to have to save her," a voice said behind him.

He spun around, his heart pounding. In front of him stood four or five of the Terracotta Warriors. "This dream just went from weird to completely strange," Nick said.

"You know how to survive the booby traps," one of the warriors said. "Your dissertation, remember?"

Nick stared at the two-thousand-year-old stone warrior statue that was reminding him about his unfinished dissertation. Man, as soon as he woke up, he would have to find a shrink for sure.

"Well?" the warrior asked.

"Sure," Nick said. "In theory, survival is told in the four Confucian proverbs that Emperor Huangdi spoke on his deathbed. But that is only in theory, and how the hell did you know about my dissertation?"

The stone warriors all glanced at each other, puzzled. Then one said, *"Everyone* knows about the Scholar From Above."

"Scholar From—" Nick suddenly knew what they were talking about. They thought he was the Scholar told about in the Monkey King myth. Fat chance of that.

"Look," he said to the stone warriors, "the Confucian proverb thing is just a theory. If I were wrong, we could both die in there."

"Will you take that chance?" one warrior asked.

Nick shook his head in disbelief. "I'm going to wake up soon, I know it. I should just walk right out and never—"

"And never see her again," another warrior said.

The image of her beautiful smile, the sound

of her fantastic laugh, came clearly back to his mind. He could feel himself being pulled toward the shimmering light. He couldn't let her die in there.

"This is just crazy." He turned to face the colors that filled the end of the tunnel.

"Follow your heart, Scholar," one of the warriors behind him said. "Or you will curse yourself for the rest of your life."

"Yeah, right." Nick shook his head. What a bunch of hooey. But the image of her looking into his eyes was too much to shove away. If one of the unopened tombs really was beyond that light, he couldn't let her be in there alone.

He took a deep breath. "Man, how stupid is this?"

Luckily, no warriors answered him.

He stepped into the light.

He wasn't sure what he expected, but it certainly wasn't what happened.

Nothing.

Exactly nothing happened.

He didn't feel the light as he passed through, and even on the other side, there was only more dirt corridor heading off as far as the light would shine.

And no sign of her.

"Hello?" His voice echoed a little and then was swallowed by the tunnel. "Where are you?"

More damned nothing.

Behind him, the light from the shimmering wall slowly vanished, transforming the entrance back into a dirt wall. The corridor ahead was lit by a faint glow coming from the soil.

"Looks like I'm stuck now." Nick patted the dirt where the shimmering light had been a few moments before. "Nowhere to go but forward, it seems."

He turned and looked down the corridor. "OK, let's see if I can remember the four proverbs of Confucius."

He started forward. Then, as he put his right foot down, he remembered the first proverb: *"With fear and trembling, as though on the edge of a Great Abyss!"*

He was almost too late. Tiny fissure lines formed in the ground under his right foot, as if he had stepped on some very thin ice. Luckily he had stopped before putting all his weight on his right foot. He leaned back, balancing all his weight on his left foot. Around him, the cracks spread like glass breaking in slow motion.

Quickly hunks of ground fell away, revealing a blackness below that seemed to have no bottom. More than likely there was a bottom, just a very long way down.

The wall of the tunnel also cracked and fell away around him. It seemed the entire corridor had been built to fall apart.

Dust swirled and dirt rained on his head as he stood, all his weight on his left foot as he tried not to fall.

So this was happening to him. Why hadn't this happened to her as well?

Finally, when everything around him was gone and the dust settled, he looked around. He was now balanced on a razor-thin ridge of dirt that seemed to stretch off into the distance in front of him like a line on a highway. There was nothing around him but blackness, both above and on both sides of the thin edge of ground he was standing on.

He eased his right foot down on the ridge and got his balance just as he heard a whooshing sound growing louder and louder.

"Next proverb," he said out loud, trying to remember it while not allowing himself to look down into the blackness.

In the distance fiery points of light were swirling and coming closer.

"Next proverb," Nick said to himself, forcing himself to think, to remember.

"The righteous man is like the North Star . . ."

The first point of light became a fireball and exploded into the thin ridge on his right, shaking him.

Another slammed into the ridge on his left, even closer.

And there were more coming.

Many more.

". . . which remains in its place while the lesser stars pay tribute."

He froze himself in place as more and more of the fireballs slammed into the ridge. "Stay put, Nick, old boy," he said. "No place to run anyway."

The onslaught was over almost as soon as it had begun. But now, instead of standing on a long ridge line, he was atop a rather fragile-looking stone column. Next to him was another column.

And beyond that was another and another,

each with a flat top not much bigger than a piece of typing paper.

"Third proverb." This time, he remembered it clearly. *"The gentleman does not rest until after he has leaped ahead."*

He looked at the distance to the next stone column. It wasn't much farther than his longest stride, but the top of the column couldn't be any wider than his size eleven shoes.

He took a deep breath and crouched slightly. "Why didn't I do this when I was twenty?"

He jumped to the next precipice, the ground crumbling under his foot as he landed.

"Take your time," he said to himself as he caught his balance and exhaled. "There's no need to panic."

But the moment the words left his lips, he knew they were wrong. The column was starting to crumble away under the pressure of his weight.

He sized up the next column top and jumped again.

This one felt no more solid than the last the moment he caught his balance again.

"I hate Emperor Huangdi." He jumped again.

He had no idea how many jumps he made until finally one column seemed to be solid under his feet. He raised his arms over his head to try to catch his breath, and banged his hand on the sky.

"What?"

He looked closer at what was ahead of him. The sky and the rest of the columns were painted onto the chamber walls, an illusion he would have bought if he hadn't stopped to rest.

Suddenly two portals appeared in front of him on the wall. The first was a doorway, dropping into some sort of pit on the other side. The other led to a staircase, wide and very solid-looking, that appeared to lead up to the surface light.

"Nice trick." Under his feet, the column started to crumble.

Nick remembered clearly the last proverb. *"Who expects to exit by any other means than . . ."*

The column disintegrated as Nick jumped.

". . . the door."

He was almost too late. He barely made the leap, grabbing the lower edge of the door and rolling himself up and through the opening.

But there was nothing solid on the other side, and the next instant he found himself sliding on his stomach, headfirst down a slick black tunnel. No matter how hard he tried, he couldn't slow himself down.

Ahead there was a light.

The end of the tunnel.

"I hope it's soft!" he shouted.

His hope was for naught. The tunnel emptied him out of what looked like the sky right over a grass-covered miniature mountain. He landed hard on the slope and kept sliding and tumbling, banging into rocks and limbs until finally coming to a very abrupt stop against the trunk of a tree.

All he could do was moan.

Over his head a bird flittered in the branches, making a chirping noise.

Carefully, he tried to move, checking for broken bones. Above him the sun was warm, and around him mountain flowers were in full bloom in arrays of colors like nothing Nick had ever seen.

He moved one leg, then the other.

Nothing broken.

His arms and back seemed fine as well, so he slowly pushed himself to his feet.

He was going to be very, very sore tomorrow.

Around him, the world went on as if he hadn't even arrived. Only there didn't seem to be any people around.

"Hello!" he shouted. His voice echoed off pear trees heavy with fruit. "Hello!"

"Scholar!" a voice shouted back.

It wasn't the voice of the woman he had hoped to save, but a deep, nasal voice that seemed almost too loud for such an open area.

"Well," the voice said, "all I can say is it is about time."

Nick looked around behind the tree he had hit and there, trapped under the mountain, his lower half pinned in the exact same pose as the classical Chinese painting, was a creature half-man, half-monkey.

The real Monkey King in all his furry flesh.

Nick opened his mouth to say something, but no words came out.

"Now get me out of here," Monkey said. "We have work to do."

Five

Nick paced back and forth in front of the mountain that was holding the Monkey King captive, trying to take stock on just where he was. The wonderful smell of spring surrounded him. Flowers he had never seen were in bloom, birds chirped in the trees, and the sky overhead was a perfect blue.

In the distance, the countryside dropped away into the mists, a picture-perfect image.

Too perfect.

"I don't believe any of this," Nick said to Monkey. "Where's that girl? I didn't even get her real name. Did she survive?"

"You'll meet her soon enough," Monkey said, "so long as you get to work and fulfill your destiny."

"And what do you know about my destiny?" Nick asked, standing over the half-man, half-monkey creature being held by a mountain that looked perfectly formed, yet couldn't have been more than five stories tall.

"I'm the Monkey King," the creature said. "I know just about everything."

"Wait a minute," Nick said. "You're saying

you are the real Monkey King?" He laughed.
"I sure don't know what that guy put in those
martinis, but—"

"You're the Scholar From Above, right?"

"No, my name is Nicholas Orton."

"You didn't write *In Search of the Monkey
King*?"

Nick looked hard at the black eyes of the
creature. The name had shocked him. "That
was supposed to be the title of my dissertation
back in college. How did you—"

"Supposed to be?" Monkey shouted. Above
him the mountain rumbled.

"I never finished it," Nick said, not wanting
to defend himself to this creature. "I changed
my major to business ten years ago, then went
to work for a corporation."

Monkey shook his head in disbelief. "That
explains why you're ten years late."

"It does?" Nick tried his best to not be defensive. He had gotten a lot of criticism from
all sides when he quit, and he didn't need more
now in this dream or drugged state or wherever
he was.

"Sure," Monkey said. "You were supposed to
have finished *In Search of the Monkey King*, then
lead an expedition down here to find the lost
manuscript. That's how your world gets saved.
It was such a great plan. I can't believe you
messed it up."

Monkey looked clearly disgusted—at least as
disgusted as a half-man, half-monkey could look
while being pinned down under a miniature
mountain.

"What's wrong with my world?" Nick asked, remembering earlier when the radio tower had vanished.

"You haven't noticed?" Monkey asked, his voice filled with so much sarcasm he almost spit the last word. "By now clocks should already be running backward."

Nick glanced down at his watch, which was running backward again.

"Things aren't going to get any better, either, until you find *Journey to the West* and return it to safety."

Nick shook his head. This was just too much to take. It was as if he were back in college and having a bad dream right before an important final. But this dream didn't seem to be going away.

"Let's start with the basics, shall we?" Nick said, trying to clear his mind. "Where am I?"

"You're inside the Emperor Huangdi's underground tomb," Monkey said, "the one in which he recreated all of China." Monkey patted the bulk that was holding him captive. "Mountains and all."

Nick looked around at the mountains in the distance, obscured by mist under the gentle sun.

"Here the spirits and deities of the Middle Kingdom now reside," Monkey said.

Suddenly Monkey's strange face transformed into an ageless warrior spirit that kept talking in Monkey's rough voice. "*Journey to the West* was stolen centuries ago by demons who put a spell on it, potent enough to destroy the book after five hundred years."

"The spell takes five hundred years to destroy one book?" Nick asked as Monkey changed back into the half-and-half state.

"It is a very powerful book," Monkey said.

"Yeah, right."

"If the demons succeed in destroying that manuscript, the world as you know it will cease to exist."

"So if I believe all this," Nick said, "just when is this five hundred years up?"

"Oh." Monkey looked contemplative. "Right around this Thursday."

"What?"

"See why you should have come here ten years ago?" Monkey said, clearly disgusted. "The Scholar From Above must rescue the sacred manuscript and deliver it to safety."

"Are you insane?" Nick asked. "I'm not even a scholar anymore. I'm in business."

"Business?" Monkey spat the word. "What's that? What do you sell? Shoes?"

Nick waved both hands in frustration at Monkey. "I don't have time for this. I've got the biggest meeting of my career tomorrow. All I want to know is where did that girl go?"

"Will you stop thinking about that girl?" Monkey said. "I'm the one you're here to free, remember?"

Nick laughed, smiling down at Monkey. "I'll get you out once you tell me how to find her."

Monkey sighed and then shook his head.

"Did anyone ever tell you that you have a one-track mind?"

"Fine," Nick said. "Have it your way. I'll find her myself."

He turned his back on Monkey and headed around the mountain and into some thick trees.

He was disgusted. He hadn't risked his life in Emperor Huangdi's little funhouse for the sake of an old book or a talking monkey.

Nick stopped at a sound above him. On the slope about a hundred paces up the hill was a very large, very hungry-looking tiger. The thing had to be five times Nick's size.

Nick stopped, frozen. Maybe he should re-think finding the woman. If he remembered his myths correctly, the Monkey King was to be the protector for the Scholar. Right about now he needed some protection, whether he was the Scholar or not.

He took a slow step backward as the tiger growled low and mean.

"Nice kitty," Nick said.

The tiger growled again. It clearly did not like being called *kitty*.

"To hell with this." Nick turned and ran like crazy out of the brush. As he reached Monkey, he glanced around, but luckily the tiger wasn't following him. At least not yet.

"All right," Nick said, looking at the trapped Monkey. "How do I get you out of there?"

Monkey picked at the fur on his side casually, as if not really paying any attention. "I didn't hear you say you were sorry."

"All right, all right," Nick said as the brush rustled where the tiger was. "I'm sorry."

"For acting like a . . ." Monkey was clearly prompting him to say something he wanted to hear.

"Like an unenlightened being."

Monkey snorted. "Try like an asshole."

At that moment the tiger came out of the shrubs, clearly not in any hurry to pounce. But there was no doubt in Nick's mind that it would pounce—and very soon.

"Break the seal," Monkey said, casually pointing up the mountain.

"The what?"

"Break the seal," Monkey said, "like the Tang Priest did in *Journey to the West.*"

Nick looked up at where a strip of ribbon covered with glowing red ideographs had been pasted over the mountain summit like a piece of tape holding the top together. "I've got to make it all the way to the top? With that thing on my tail?"

Nick pointed at the tiger, which only smiled and licked its lips. To it, Nick was clearly dinner.

"Well, you have a weapon, don't you?" Monkey asked.

The tiger crouched to pounce as Nick reached into his pocket and came up with his cell phone.

He hurled it as hard as he could at the tiger, hitting the cat directly on the nose. The cat backed up, stunned that someone would do something so stupid.

It was the only diversion Nick was going to

get. He turned and, as fast as he could run, scrambled up the side of the miniature mountain.

About halfway up, he glanced back to see the tiger starting up after him.

"Shit, shit, shit," Nick said. "How did I get into this? Time to wake up!"

After another fifty steps, he again glanced back. The tiger was climbing without any effort and was gaining fast.

"Monkey!" Nick shouted as he ran.

"What?" Monkey's voice floated up over the rocks and grass of the mountain slopes.

"A little help!" Nick shouted back. He was only twenty steps from the top and the red ribbon, but he wasn't going to make it.

"Well, all right," Monkey said, again his voice carrying clearly.

Suddenly the ground under Nick seemed to heave upward. Rocks rained down from near the summit, pelting both Nick and the tiger not more than ten paces behind.

The tiger growled in anger and stopped, not happy with all the rocks and shaking ground.

Nick, on his hands and knees, kept scrambling for the bright red tape.

Finally it was in his grasp. He took a handful of the soft ribbon and yanked hard, ripping the seal of heaven from the top of the mountain.

The ground calmed and Nick glanced over his shoulder as the tiger crouched, ready to pounce on him.

"Monkey!" Nick shouted.

The tiger leaped, and Nick started to cover

his head. Suddenly the ground between him and the tiger erupted like a water main had blown under it. The explosion caught the tiger in mid leap, sending the startled cat upward at least a hundred feet.

Nick pulled himself up onto a big rock and sat down just as the cat flipped over and somehow managed to land on its feet.

From inside the rock, where the explosion had happened, Monkey's voice sounded. "The Great Sage Equaling Heaven springs forth once more to amaze and delight all Creation."

The hole in the mountain widened.

"Can we get a fanfare?" Monkey asked.

Nick expected music to come out of the ground, but there was nothing. Only Monkey, who sprang into the air at least twice as high as the tiger had gone, landing easily on his feet right in front of the big beast.

The tiger crouched and again growled, clearly about to pounce on Monkey.

Monkey pulled a tiny needle from behind his ear. "Grow."

The needle expanded into Monkey's legendary weapon, the gold-banded cudgel. Nick had seen pictures of it in the books and murals, but he had never expected to see it in real life—if this could be called real life.

Monkey spun the cudgel in a display of martial arts that would have impressed Bruce Lee. The tiger simply watched, clearly wondering what its dinner was doing.

Finally, Monkey tired of the routine and

reached out and rapped the unsuspecting cat on the nose.

The tiger howled, turned, and ran.

Monkey shrank the cudgel back to its storage size and replaced it behind his ear. Then he turned to face Nick, smiling.

"Thank you." Nick brushed off his pants as he stood.

"For what?"

"For saving my life."

"I'm sure it won't be the last time." Monkey turned and headed down the hill. "Come on. The demon and monsters are this way."

"But where is *she?*" Nick demanded. She had asked him to trust her. As far as he was concerned, it was about time she showed her face.

"You are giving me an orangutan-sized headache." Monkey stopped and looked back up at Nick. "It's time to begin the pilgrimage. Actually, we should have started ten years ago, but we won't talk about that."

"Who said I was going on any pilgrimage?" Nick asked. He wasn't moving unless that tiger came back.

"Fine. You don't care about your world, why should I?" Monkey shook his head in disgust and stomped ten feet off, then came back.

"How in Buddha's name was I ever supposed to teach someone as shallow as you?"

Again Monkey turned and marched off as the setting sun saturated the hills in deep scarlet.

"You were supposed to be my *teacher?*" Nick laughed.

Monkey stopped. "It is the greatest honor a

soul can attain: the title of Teacher. But no one could succeed with a student like you."

Monkey stormed back toward Nick, then motioned with his wrist and pointed to something behind Nick. He glanced around to see a golden pagoda floating in midair just beyond the peak of the mountain. A flight of shimmering stairs led from its portal to the ground.

"See those stairs?" Monkey asked, pointing at what he had just made appear. "They'll lead you back to the Terracotta Warriors. Go home. I give up on you."

Nick glanced at the stairs, then back at the Monkey King.

"There is no Scholar From Above," Monkey said. "Or if there ever was, he died a long time ago."

"Trust me," Nick said, facing Monkey, "I'll be glad to head up those stairs and just leave you alone if you tell me if she is all right."

Monkey snorted. "She's fine. Better than you'll ever be."

"Then can I see her?"

"Get those ideas out of your head." Monkey stepped toward Nick with a very menacing look in his eyes. Nick held his ground and Monkey stopped. "Listen, salesman, she is way, *way* out of your league."

Nick had no doubt that was true. "She is perfect, isn't she?"

Monkey snorted again. "No, I mean she's a goddess."

"Yeah, she is," Nick agreed, smiling, remembering her smile, her laugh, her soft touch.

"You are dumber than you look, and that's going some. Don't you get it? A goddess. Literally."

"What?"

In the distance, Nick could hear a Chinese opera aria, like a distant siren's call. Above them, a golden light opened up the skies, growing in intensity.

"You ever hear of Kwan Ying?" He pointed up. "Now I'm in big trouble, and it's all your fault."

Nick was slowly starting to understand. But his mind didn't want to grasp what Monkey was saying. "Kwan Ying? You mean the Goddess of Mercy?"

In the golden light above, Kwan Ying suddenly appeared, floating slowly downward. She was dressed just as Nick had last seen her, in the silks and large headdress.

"The cloud under her feet oughta be a dead giveaway," Monkey said.

Nick watched in awe as she landed right in front of him.

"At the moment," Kwan said, "I do not feel like a goddess." She looked Nick right in the eyes. "I must ask your forgiveness for luring you here this way."

All Nick wanted to do was stare at her. As far as he was concerned, he could stare at her the rest of his life. She was that beautiful. But after a moment he forced himself to answer her. "Well, at least this explains a few things. Your drinking habits, for starters."

She giggled, the sound like a million children laughing. Nick could tell she was pleased.

"You have no idea how difficult it is to drink and fly at the same time."

He laughed with her, like two friends sharing an old memory. Behind her Monkey just stared at them, completely shocked, which made Nick feel even better.

Kwan cleared her throat and tried to resume her Mother Mary-like bearing, but Nick could see the twinkle in her eye and the slight curl at the corner of her mouth.

"I thought we were having a good time," Nick said. "That wasn't a lie, was it?"

She blushed at the question and then smiled at him. "You know the answer to that as well as I do."

That made Nick's heart leap. She had felt the same way he had.

"Goddess," Monkey said, disgusted at what he was seeing, "you don't know this guy. He's impossible."

Kwan turned to Monkey. "You've worked so hard for a chance to become a teacher. Will you give up on him so easily?"

"He's arrogant, headstrong, and, worst of all, he doesn't even *want* to learn."

Nick just stared at Monkey, as if the creature were talking about someone else instead of him. Those traits didn't sound at all like he felt inside.

Kwan smiled at Monkey. "Neither did you," she said, "when Tang Priest first became your teacher."

Monkey looked stunned. "Me? You can't possibly be comparing me to—" With a dismissive wave, Monkey indicated Nick. Nick just smiled.

Kwan looked at Monkey and nodded.

"But I was brilliant!" Monkey shouted.

"So is he."

Nick blushed. Learning that she thought he was brilliant had just made his day. Maybe his entire month. No, it was enough for a full year.

"He's a salesman!" Monkey almost shouted. "I know you're the Goddess of Mercy, but you can't—"

Kwan placed her palms together and began to chant. A moment later, a beam of light radiated from her forehead, bathing Monkey.

Almost instantly Monkey's anger vanished and he rolled on the ground like a contented puppy.

"Ohh," he said, "I love it when you do that."

She turned back to Nick.

"That was amazing." Nick stared at Monkey, then at Kwan.

"Just part of the job," she said, smiling at him.

Nick glanced at Monkey again, then faced Kwan directly. "Listen, I hate to admit it, but Monkey's right about a few things. You saw me in my world. I'm not exactly the hero type."

"No?" she asked, the twinkle again back in her eye and the smile easing onto her wonderful lips. "Who pushed me from the path of a speeding truck?"

Now the smile was back completely as she

went on. "And who refused to take advantage
of a girl who drank too many martinis?"

"Well, I thought about it," Nick said, laughing. "Doesn't that count against me?"

She laughed, then said, "Whether you decide
to help us or not, I will always remember you
with a smile." She pointed to Nick's right. "Let
me show you something."

An image of an elderly Chinese man dressed
in Ming dynasty robes and sitting at a table appeared on a rock outcropping.

"This man," Kwan said, "lived five hundred
years ago, in the world of humans above. His
name was Wu Cheng-En."

Nick was shocked. "He wrote *Journey to the
West.*"

Kwan smiled at Nick, obviously pleased he
knew that. She offered her hand to him and
he took it, enjoying again the wonderful feel of
her skin against his.

"Come," she said. "Let me take you into his
world."

Nick would have gone anywhere with her for
just about any reason.

They moved up the slope to where the image
filled the rock above them.

She smiled at him and then stepped into the
rock and through it to the world beyond, pulling him with her to a place that had not existed
for five hundred years.

Six

Nick expected to step into the study of the old writer, but instead he found himself still holding Kwan's hand. They were standing on a dirt road. Billowing smoke obscured the setting sun, and the smell of rot and death hung heavy around them. In front of him was a small retreat of about ten huts. From what Nick could tell, a terrible battle had left the pavilions of this village burning.

Kwan looked around and shuddered, her hand growing cold in his. "It was a time of senseless cruelty and repression."

A bonfire was roaring in the middle of the buildings as Kwan and Nick moved closer. Papers and desks were being burned and bodies were strewn everywhere. Nick had never seen bodies like this. Many of them were headless and hacked bloody. The smell of blood and shit mixed with the smoke.

As they approached, Imperial soldiers, the strongest and meanest-looking things Nick had ever seen, dragged a trembling scholar from a charred building. They forced the poor man, his hands and arms burnt, to his knees in the blood-soaked courtyard.

"Shortly before this time, the Emperor had declared all progress must cease," Kwan told Nick, clearly not worried anyone would see or hear them. "China was forced to return to the values and traditions of the past."

"I've heard that before."

"Nothing like this period," Kwan said. "Authors were only allowed to retell old tales over and over again. Their work was rigidly policed by censors led by an evil man named Shu Chung-Shing."

As Nick watched, the soldiers delivered a manuscript to a rotund man Nick assumed was Shu. The fat man glanced at it with disdain, then hurled the entire thing into the bonfire.

"Tough critic," Nick said, more to himself than Kwan.

"Shu made certain no one wrote any new stories on pain of death."

As Nick watched, soldiers raised their swords and slashed down on the scholar, cutting off his head.

Nick started forward to try to stop them, but before he could take a step, Kwan had shifted them to a new place. Now they were inside the aging Wu's study. It smelled of wood fire and old paper, and Nick could hear the faint whisper of Wu's brush-pen. The scene they had just left was like a bad memory; fresh, but not present.

Nick held his breath, worried for a moment

that the old writer would know they were there. But he didn't.

"All his life," Kwan said, "Wu had tried to obey the censors. "But when he grew old, he decided to set down the tales he had heard from the common people."

Nick moved a step forward without letting go of Kwan's hand and tried to study what Wu was writing.

"He wrote about a naughty monkey god and his adventures helping a Tang priest." Kwan pulled Nick back beside her.

Wu sat back and looked at his work, chuckling. Nick was glad the old man had liked what he wrote.

"The book he has just finished he called *Journey to the West,*" Kwan said.

As Nick watched, Wu added a bright red seal to the cover page, blew on the ink to dry it, and then stood to go to bed.

Again Kwan changed location on them.

"Would you warn me the next time you're going to do that?" Nick said as he looked around the large dining hall filled with Ming opulence and more food than Nick could ever imagine on one table. The wonderful smells of meats and sauces reminded him he hadn't eaten in what seemed like centuries.

"Sorry." Kwan squeezed his hand.

"Shu?" Nick pointed at a fat man sitting at the head of the table.

"Yes." A man entered the room and moved up beside Shu. "And the others eating with him were called the Seven Traditional Masters. Shu heard from spies about Wu's forbidden book."

"Kill him and take his manuscript," Shu told the man who entered. "Bring it to me."

"Changing now," Kwan said.

"Thank you." Suddenly they were standing in the gutter watching Wu walk past. He was carrying a package under one arm and seemed very happy with himself.

"Can't we warn him?" Nick asked.

Kwan patted his arm and never let go of his hand. "We can change the present, even the future, but never the past."

"Good words to live by," Nick said, "except in time-traveling cases like this."

Kwan said nothing.

As they watched, three large men jumped from an alley onto the author, kicking and beating him until Nick could no longer watch.

"Wu gave up his life that night for his writing," Kwan said. "Shifting."

Nick said nothing. More than anything, he wanted to be anywhere else. The images of Wu being killed for simply writing a book would stay with him for the rest of his days.

Around them the light seemed to vanish. The smell of death and mold and rot washed in so fast that Nick felt his stomach twist.

In front of them, Shu and his gang were gathered, trying to destroy Wu's manuscript. Nick watched as one poured steaming acid on it. The acid ran off.

Shu screamed and grabbed the manuscript,

tossing it into the fire. The thing sat on the coals, refusing to be consumed by the flames.

"Tough paper," Nick said.

Kwan did not laugh. "Shu could not destroy it. And there was one other thing Shu had not counted on."

The scene shifted without warning and Nick and Kwan were entering an unkempt garden filled with dense, overgrown shrubs and brush. Behind the brush was a small shed. Inside, a printer worked at a secret press, arranging thousands of wood blocks.

"Wu had already delivered an early draft of his book to an underground printer," Kwan said, pointing through an opening at the man working. "So *Journey to the West* was published, despite Shu's terrible efforts."

"Seems to me," Nick said, "that the story has a happy ending. What do you need me for?"

The scene in the garden slowly vanished, to be replaced with them back in the world of spirits, near the top of the small mountain where Nick had had his run-in with the tiger. Monkey was still on the ground, smiling and rolling around, as if having the best dream possible.

"Shu and his masters found that only a five-hundred-year spell could destroy Wu's manuscript," Kwan said. "Now those five hundred years have almost passed, and *Journey to the West* is on the verge of disappearing forever."

She looked into Nick's eyes, and suddenly he started to understand a little more. "Wait. You mean those censors are still alive?"

Kwan nodded. "Their spirits live on, as demons, here in our world below."

"What kind of world is this, anyway?" Nick glanced around at the picture-perfect Chinese landscape that surrounded them. Night was almost on them, but he could still see details of trees and mountains and faint mists floating over valleys.

"All the legendary figures of Chinese history and myth come here after their deaths," Kwan said, "to join the souls of the ordinary Chinese buried with the Emperor."

She looked directly at Nick. "Only a human can carry the manuscript back to safety in your world, where it belongs."

Nick shook his head. "I just don't get it, I guess," he said. "You guys are putting all this time and energy into worrying about a book. Why?"

For the first time since he had met her, he could tell Kwan was angry. A touch of fire seemed to flicker around the edges of her eyes. He wanted to let go of her hand and step back, but he didn't.

"Not just any book, Nicholas Orton."

He knew when she used his full name, he was in big trouble.

She looked up and overhead stars appeared, thousands of them, bright pinpoints of light filling the sky.

Kwan took a deep breath, seeming to gather energy from the sudden appearance of the stars. "There are some books so powerful that their very existence changed the world. The

Bible, the Koran, the teachings of Buddha. These writings have fueled human progress and change."

She looked at him directly, her anger gone. "Shu and the Masters are trying to remove one such book from your world."

"But it's published everywhere." Nick suddenly remembered that in the marketplace, she had shown him a copy with the words vanishing.

"Now you understand," Kwan said. "This is a special book. All copies are tied to the original. If it is destroyed, all copies in your world will vanish. It is the power of the Masters and Shu."

"And the radio tower?" Nick asked, fearing he knew what she would say.

"When the book is gone, as if it never had been, then all the progress the book inspired will also be gone."

"Clocks running backward," Nick said, beginning to understand.

Kwan nodded, a great sadness in her eyes. "Shu and his Masters will have finally achieved the goal that eluded them in their lifetimes. They will have eliminated all human progress and return your world to the way it was during the heyday of ancient China."

The weight of what she was saying finally sunk into Nick's thick skull. He glanced down at his watch. The second hand was running backward. He took a deep breath and looked back up at her. He had one very important question left.

"Why me? Aren't there others who could help?"

"You are the Scholar From Above." Kwan squeezed his hand. "Your coming was foretold hundreds of years ago."

"Too bad someone didn't tell me, say, ten years ago."

Kwan smiled. "Buddha himself decreed that one day a human would discover the means to enter our world, and in so doing, that Scholar would also save his own."

"Buddha?" Nick said, more shocked than he had been.

"Don't you understand?" Kwan said. "You have always had a gift."

She again waved a hand, and the image on the rock changed into a picture of his younger self. Nick stared at the image of the days when he was in college, his nose buried completely in a Chinese manuscript. It brought back memories he had been trying to put away for years.

"You believed then," Kwan said, "that if Eastern and Western wisdom could somehow come together, people might find a better way to live."

"I gave all that up," Nick said. "No one really cared about dusty manuscripts and dead Chinese writers."

Kwan looked at him as if he were a child. "You cannot lie to me, even though you do to yourself. You gave up when someone broke your heart."

The memory of the last night with Linda, his first love, flashed through his mind, then vanished. He was good at making the pain go away, and this moment was just another of many.

The image of his younger self vanished.

Nick turned to her. "You gods really do your homework."

"Broken hearts can always be mended." Kwan smiled at him. "So long as you are willing to take a chance."

He could feel every ounce of his resistance melting into that smile. If it meant being with Kwan longer, he'd do anything. She was the chance he wanted to take.

They held the gaze for a few long moments. Again he felt like leaning forward and kissing her, as long and as passionately as he could manage.

Suddenly Monkey let out a shriek and jumped to his feet. "That was great!" he said, rubbing his hands together. "I'm ready to teach, teach, teach." He moved up beside Nick and looked him right in the eye. "How about it, salesman? Let's go defeat some evil."

Nick smiled at Monkey, then back at Kwan. "What about my meeting?"

Kwan put her palms together and a light fanned out from her willowy form. "Howsoever long your pilgrimage may take down here, in your world above, it will be as if only one night had passed."

Nick laughed. "You have a solution for almost anything." He glanced at Monkey. "All right, I'll do it."

She leaned forward and touched his forehead. Before he could kiss her or even touch her hand again, a cloud gathered under her feet and she lifted into the air.

"Did that mean I'll be seeing you around?" Nick shouted up at her.

She laughed. "Just whisper a prayer. I will always be with you, Nicholas Orton."

She moved up and up until finally she became just another star in the sky.

"Call me Nick," he said softly, staring at where she had gone.

"You think she likes you?" Monkey asked, clearly making fun of Nick.

"Maybe." Nick glanced at the half-monkey, half-human. "Is that so hard to believe?"

"In a word, yes," Monkey said. "But do yourself a favor and don't take it personally. Romantic love makes a warrior weak, and we don't have time for it."

"Don't worry about me," Nick replied. "I gave up love a long time ago."

"Good." Monkey offered Nick his paw-like hand. "Let's see what you are made of."

As soon as Nick took Monkey's paw, they shot skyward, with Nick hanging on for dear life. Traveling with Kwan was a much saner experience, that was for sure.

"You all right?" Monkey asked as he bounded lightly from dark cloud to dark cloud through the night sky.

Nick managed to nod.

"Great!" Monkey shouted to Nick. "First stop, the Monkey Kingdom."

Seven

Monkey finally settled down on one cloud, moving it forward through the night sky. Nick was amazed that the cloud felt so solid under his feet. He had decided in the first few seconds of being there that he wasn't going to question it. No doubt that questioning things in this strange place, especially anything to do with reality, was often the wrong thing to do. But he was standing on a cloud that was being steered through the night by a half-monkey, half-human, and that was going to take some getting used to.

"So why are we headed to your Kingdom first?" Nick tried to make himself relax by sitting down next to Monkey.

"When I was imprisoned under that mountain," Monkey said, "Shu swore he'd destroy my kingdom. I must go see my subjects."

"Oh."

"I'm glad you agree." Monkey stood and pulled Nick to his feet. "Time for your first lesson." He removed the pin from behind his ear and said, "Grow."

Nick watched as Monkey then whispered,

"Change" to the grown cudgel. It produced a copy of itself.

"Here." Monkey tossed Nick the duplicate, then began spinning and whirling around, almost faster than the eye could follow.

"All the other gods laughed when I said I would become a teacher. How hard could it be? I tell you what to do, you do it."

Nick managed not to say anything. Instead, he just stared at the heavy weapon in his hand. He couldn't seem to find a way even to hold it without being afraid he might cut himself.

Monkey became even more of a blur, talking the entire time. "Enemy here, chop there. Behind, pow! Two: swing then chop. An army after you, flip, turn, somersault, strike, strike, swing, strike."

Monkey stopped and looked squarely at Nick. "OK. Any questions?"

Nick held the cudgel up, barely keeping it from slicing into his shoulder. "Yeah. How do you hold it?"

Monkey blinked at Nick as if seeing him for the very first time.

"We'll continue the lesson tomorrow," Monkey said.

The duplicate cudgel snapped out of Nick's hands and disappeared into Monkey's grasp.

"Look," Monkey said as the cloud approached the slowly increasing light area that indicated the sun was coming back up in this strange place. "There's my kingdom."

As the island came into view, Nick carefully moved to the edge of the solid-feeling cloud

and leaned over, straining to see what it looked
like. Entire valleys, once clearly lush with tropi-
cal vegetation, appeared as if they had been
strip-mined. Everything looked brown and
dead.

On the shore of a pond formed by a waterfall,
Nick could see several dozen monkey-like creatures dressed in rags, struggling to gather a very
sad-looking crop.

"My children . . ." Monkey's loud and strong
voice was no more than a whisper.

Nick glanced at the sad, shocked look on the
Monkey King's face. It almost made Nick like
the guy. Almost.

The next instant the cloud dropped toward
the land like a stone, and Nick held on for dear
life, hoping against hope he wouldn't be the
first recorded fatality of a cloud-island collision.

They didn't hit. It seemed Monkey, even
when upset, could drive a cloud perfectly. The
white puff leveled off fifty feet above the
ground and seemed to hover.

Monkey leaped off, leaving Nick alone on the
cloud and landed on the shore of the pond, his
arms outstretched in regal authority. "My subjects," Monkey said, his voice carrying over the
dead hills and into the ruined valleys, "your
handsome Monkey has returned."

Nick's cloud moved lower and lower as a few
of Monkey's subjects moved toward their king.

"Look who decided to pay us a visit," one
subject said.

"Maybe we should offer him something to

eat," another said. "Oh, wait, I remember now. We haven't eaten in weeks."

A female monkey looked at him and shook her finger. "You say you're going out for coconut milk, then disappear for almost five hundred years."

Clearly things were not going well for Monkey on his return. At that moment Nick's cloud bumped into a low hill next to the pond and he climbed off. The moment he did, the cloud shimmered and vanished.

"Will you all please shut up?" Monkey shouted as more and more complaints flooded at him.

"Look, I don't blame you for being upset," Monkey said to his people. "I'm angry, too. I've just spent the last five hundred years imprisoned beneath the Five-Element Mountain."

The monkeys listening to him recoiled in horror and surprise. One said, "No wonder he didn't come back."

"Yeah," another said. "Makes sense."

Monkey went on, his voice gaining power and anger. "I was left there by the same demons who destroyed our land and reduced you to misery: Shu and the Seven Traditional Masters. But now we will make this bootlicker Shu pay tenfold for the crimes he has committed."

Monkey raised his fist in the air. "Let us go to find Shu! Vengeance is ours!"

Nick was moved. The monkeys weren't.

"It's not Shu," one subject said from the front of the group.

"Excuse me?" Monkey said.

"He's right," another said, as more and more of them nodded. "It's not Shu who destroyed our land."

"Then who was it?" Monkey demanded.

Almost as one they turned and pointed toward the pond. Nick followed where they were pointing, and could see a cave entrance visible behind the waterfall.

"The Demon Prince of Confusion," a few of them said together.

"That's right," another said. "He's taken our wonderful cave and stolen our children."

Monkey stared at his people, then glanced over at Nick before looking back at his people. "The Prince of Confusion?"

Nick could tell that was not what Monkey expected to hear.

Everyone nodded.

"But didn't his father, the King of Confusion, attack us a few millennia ago?"

"Yup! Yes! Sure did!" echoed from the growing crowd.

Monkey shook his head in disgust and disbelief. "I sent that amateur whimpering back with his horns between his legs. How dare his son show his scales around here?"

"Well, he had help," one subject said.

Everyone nodded.

Nick knew this was where the famous "other shoe" was going to drop.

"Yeah," one subject said, "he attacked us with an entire regiment of the Jade Emperor's own heavenly soldiers."

Again Monkey glanced at Nick, but this time Nick could see the worry in Monkey's eyes.

"The Jade Emperor's soldiers attacking my kingdom?" Monkey shook his head as if to clear it. "That just doesn't make sense. The Emperor and I made our peace long ago."

Monkey stood staring out over his people, then snorted. "Whatever is going on here, it stinks to high heaven."

He turned and headed for the waterfall at a purposeful march. "First things first. I'm going to send that spoiled brat back home to Daddy." Nick, who was standing near where Monkey was going to pass, was suddenly grabbed by Monkey and yanked into the air.

"You're with me, Salesman. Time for a lesson."

All the subjects cheered and patted each other on the back and hugged each other as if the battle was already won. Nick was more concerned about the coming landing.

Monkey's jump took them into the waterfall and then through it. They landed outside the cave entrance, where Monkey dropped Nick as if he were a bag of groceries.

Monkey shook, water flying everywhere, ending up almost instantly dry. Then he looked at Nick and his sopping wet clothes as Nick pulled himself to his feet. "You humans have got to learn to waterproof your fur."

"Yeah, right." Nick wrung some of the water from his shirt and tucked it back into his pants.

Ahead of them, in the mouth of the cave, footsteps sounded. Monkey pulled Nick behind some rocks just as two wolf-like creatures in slacks and no shirts came out. They were challenging each other by doing different, blinding-fast moves with their swords. Nick had never seen anything like it.

He glanced at Monkey. "Should we be worried?"

Monkey snorted. "Yeah, I'm gonna die laughing." He looked at Nick. "Now, watch and learn something, will ya?"

Monkey stepped from behind the rock to face the two wolf-guards, taking what Nick figured was a fighting stance.

"I am Sun Wukong!" Monkey proclaimed. "The Monkey King."

The guards stopped and stared, their wolf-like mouths hanging open in shock, saliva dripping into pools at their feet.

"Go tell your cowardly ruler the time has come for him to pay for his crimes," Monkey said, his voice echoing in the cave mouth.

Nick doubted anyone in that cave hadn't heard Monkey.

Both guards dropped into a fighting stance and moved toward Monkey, twirling their weapons around themselves like they knew what they were doing.

"Are you deaf as well as stupid?" Monkey asked.

Monkey made his cudgel grow. Then he danced around in front of them at lightning speed, twirling and spinning and thrusting and pretending to battle. He stopped and stared at the two wolf-guards, a smile on his face. "Two against one. Are those really fair odds?"

Monkey had clearly won the showmanship part of the contest.

One of the guards turned and barked back into the cave.

Monkey glanced over at Nick and smiled. "Well, so much for the guards."

As he spoke, at least two dozen more wolf-like guards came running from the cave mouth, all carrying very sharp swords. They quickly surrounded Monkey, who stood and waited until they got into position.

"Now this is a more even fight," Monkey said.

Nick watched in complete awe as Monkey moved his gold-banded cudgel in a blur of motion as three of the guards charged. Almost without effort on Monkey's part, the three were unconscious on the ground, cut and bleeding.

"Who wants to see that again?" Monkey asked as the other guards tightened the circle around him.

Five guards broke and rushed at Monkey.

Monkey jumped into the air, bringing his feet into the action as again the cudgel moved so fast Nick couldn't follow it.

Three seconds later, the five guards were piled on top of the first three, bleeding from places it wasn't natural to bleed from.

The other ten guards looked at each other, worry and terror in their eyes.

Monkey bowed and smiled. "Now a little number I call *Panic Time.*"

The rest of the guards rushed Monkey haphazardly, all the order and discipline they once had now tossed to the wind.

Again the battle was laughably short. Only one of the original guards was left standing.

"Are you ready to take that message to your leader now?" Monkey asked.

The ground shook as if there was an earthquake. Nick held onto the rock he'd been hiding behind and looked around.

"Oh, never mind." Monkey sliced off the guard's wolf-like head. "I hear him coming."

Nick looked into the cave just as a twenty-foot giant lumbered into view. His forehead was ringed with nasty-looking horns and his body was covered with what looked like a scale armor. A strong wind swirled around his head, carrying branches, rocks, and other debris. On all sides of him, staying just far enough away to be out of the wind, were thirty more of the wolf-guards.

"Monkey King," the monster said, his voice a deep roar with a wisp of wind behind it that made it sound almost sissy, "how dare you show your face to one who has sworn to destroy you?"

Monkey smiled up at the monster. "Prince of Confusion," Monkey said, "you are the spitting image of your father." Monkey shook his head as if sad. "I'm so sorry. I can only assume your mother was just as ugly. How is your old man, anyway?"

The Prince looked disgusted. "Still in two pieces, thanks to you."

Behind them, fifty guards moved to surround Nick and Monkey. Others were moving on the other side of the pond, coming from everywhere. There had to be a hundred or more. Nick stepped forward and tried to get Monkey's attention, but without luck.

"Before the sun has set," Monkey told the Prince, "you will kowtow before me and my children."

The Prince laughed, sending some sticks and rocks away from the whirlwind that surrounded his head. "Monkey, you are as arrogant as my father remembered."

"And you will tell me," Monkey said, ignoring Nick's waves to get his attention, "who in the court of the Jade Emperor enlisted heavenly soldiers to fight for a bottom-feeder like you."

"None of your business," the Prince shouted.

"Oh," Monkey said, "have I picked a sore scale?"

The Prince glanced over Monkey's head. "Why should I worry about your questions when you will no longer have a tongue to speak?"

The guards all moved at once.

"Monkey!" Nick shouted. "Behind you!"

Monkey whirled around as the wolf-like creatures charged in from all directions. Instantly Monkey jumped to Nick's side, grabbing him by the shoulders and tossing him upward into a tall tree beside the waterfall. Nick managed to grab on to a limb and swing over against the trunk. The bark was rough, but at least he wasn't coming down.

Below him Monkey stood calmly in the middle of at least a hundred charging guards, their swords stuck straight out, ready to stab Monkey from all sides.

Just as Nick was convinced his guardian was going to be sliced and diced, Monkey vanished.

The attackers ran their swords through each other.

If it hadn't been so serious, Nick would have laughed. A dozen guards fell to the ground, dead at the hands of their own men.

But now Monkey was nowhere to be seen. The guards who were still standing looked around, trying to find him. Even from Nick's perch high above the fighting, he couldn't see Monkey.

The wind around the Prince got faster and faster as he grew angrier and angrier.

Then Monkey's laugh filled the cave entrance as Monkey grew in size, right in the middle of the guards.

And again they all turned and ran at him, their swords ready to cut him.

And again he vanished as the guards cut at each other.

Over and over, Monkey popped up, then vanished. Nick was impressed.

Finally, with over half his army gone, the Prince snorted in disgust. Waving his scale-covered hand, he stirred up the wind around him into a massive tornado, which picked up Monkey and yanked Nick from his perch in the tree.

The winds were so strong that Nick found himself held up, swirling around and around the massive body of the Prince in the eye of the tornado.

"You know how to handle this?" Nick shouted to Monkey as they passed in the wind.

Monkey laughed. "His father tried the same sideshow trick."

"It seems sort of effective!" Nick shouted back.

Monkey pulled a handful of hair from his chest, held it up into the wind, and shouted, "Change!"

Each hair suddenly transformed into a tiny monkey, a replica of the Monkey King, all swirling around the Prince's head.

"No!" the Prince shouted as the monkeys started to attack him like a swarm of locusts. Slashing their tiny cudgels at his face and eyes and hands and neck, they quickly forced the Prince to his knees simply by their sheer numbers.

As he dropped, so did the intensity of the tornado holding Nick in the air. Somehow Nick managed to get himself upright and make a running landing, ending up against a large rock.

"Like father, like son," Monkey said, standing near the Prince with a sword, clearly ready to cut the Prince in half as the tiny monkeys kept up their swarming attack around the Prince's head.

Nick glanced around as the wolf-guards all backed away, clearly wanting no more of what was a losing fight.

"Please!" the Prince shouted through the swarm, "have mercy. Our families go way back."

"Who helped you acquire heavenly soldiers to attack my kingdom?"

The Prince hesitated and the little monkeys intensified their attack, cutting and stabbing with their tiny cudgels. The Prince was forced to bend even lower, and blood was flying everywhere.

"They said if I ever revealed this," the Prince spit out as little monkeys climbed in his mouth, "they would cut out my tongue."

Monkey raised the sword, ready to cut the monster in half.

"All right, all right," the Prince said.

The tiny swarm of monkeys backed off, and Nick could see the Prince's face had a thousand tiny cuts on it.

"It was Shu."

"The Shu?" Monkey asked.

"Yeah," the Prince said. "Shu and the Seven Traditional Masters. That Shu. He offered to help me avenge my father's shame."

"How filial of you," Monkey said. "But Shu and the Masters are not members of the Jade Emperor's court. Someone on the inside must've helped them get the soldiers. Who was it?"

"I don't know," the Prince said. Nick thought the big monster was about ready to break into tears. It was the most pathetic thing he had ever seen. "Shu just showed up with a regiment of heavenly troops. He never told me how he got them."

Monkey shrugged. "Wrong answer." He slowly took the sword back and got ready to cut the big monster in half. "No tongue and now no legs, either."

"I'll tell you where you can find the Masters," the Prince said, begging. "Then you can ask them yourself."

Monkey glanced at Nick, then shrugged. "Sounds like a deal."

"Their headquarters is a secret bunker on the floor of the Western Sea." The words poured out of the Prince's mouth as he stared at the sword Monkey held and at the swarm of little monkeys circling his head. "Now will you let me go?"

Monkey lowered his sword and the little monkeys jumped back into his hand.

"Change," he said.

Nick watched as they became strands of hair which Monkey stuck back into the bald place on his chest. He'd have to ask Monkey later how he did that.

"Return to the home of your father," Monkey said. "Tell him if any of your kind dare attack my children again, I will chop you all into dim sum filling."

The Prince pushed himself up to his feet, groaning, and wiped the blood from his face. "Shu said he had imprisoned you forever, that you would never return."

"Well," Monkey said, shrugging, "those who can't do, talk."

The Prince placed the fist of one hand into

the palm of his other. Nick recognized it at once as the traditional salute of respect.

"Great sage," the Prince said, "the children of your subjects I have imprisoned within the cave." The Prince waved a hand and then went on. "I free them now to rejoin their families, with my regrets for their years of slavery."

Monkey nodded toward the Prince. "You fought honorably. I accept your apology and welcome your allegiance."

Nick was shocked to see Monkey return the Prince's salute. The two stared at each other until a rumbling sound from the cave made them turn.

A moment later they were surrounded by a mass of child-monkeys, all very, very happy to be free.

Eight

Monkey and Nick slipped away from the celebration right after the Prince of Confusion and his soldiers headed off in their ship. Monkey led Nick up to a meadow just above the waterfall, where the sounds of the party could still be heard. The moment the Prince's ship had cast off, the trees leafed out, the flowers sprang from the ground, the grass grew. The island almost instantly transformed itself back into a lush paradise.

Nick had been impressed at the sudden beauty, and told Monkey so. But Monkey only shrugged. He was more intent on getting on with the mission. But first things first. He had to teach Nick how to fight.

After showing Nick how to hold the cudgel correctly, Monkey stepped back and said, "Now jump."

Nick took a step and jumped as high as he could. Back in school he had once dunked a basketball, but that was a long time ago. And the cudgel weighed a few pounds as well. But he still got what he thought was a good distance off the ground.

"No," Monkey said. "You have to turn, too."

"Then say turn."

"I just did. Turn!"

Nick took another step and jumped and turned, proud that he didn't trip when he landed.

"But use the cudgel!" Monkey ordered. "Like this!"

Monkey grabbed the cudgel from Nick's hands, turned, and jumped at least twenty feet into the air, moving the cudgel around himself in fighting motions as he came down.

"There, is that so hard?" Monkey asked.

Nick grabbed the cudgel from Monkey's hands, set himself to give the best jump he had ever done, and leaped into the air, turning as he went.

He landed with one leg twisted and managed to not cut himself with the cudgel as he sprawled on the ground.

"How are we supposed to perform our mission," Monkey asked, standing over him, "if you can't perform the simplest of tasks?"

Nick desperately wanted to punch Monkey in his pug nose, but instead he just stared up at the creature. "Because your *simple* tasks are impossible."

Monkey stared back at Nick, his anger clear. Nick didn't look away.

Finally, Monkey turned away and stormed back toward the party. An old woman walked toward them.

"We're not mad at you anymore," the granny said to Monkey as he approached, indicating the celebration going on around the pond below, "so why are you so angry?"

Monkey stopped and stared at the old woman, then said in an angry voice, "I'm supposed to teach that human." He pointed at Nick.

Nick gave Monkey the old "sit-on-it" sign.

"You?" the granny asked. "A teacher?" She burst into laughter loud enough to make Monkey step back from her.

"Sorry," she said after a moment. "For once in your life, do you think you can listen, Great Sage?"

"To you?" Monkey asked.

"To advice from an old granny, yes."

He nodded, so she went on. "You must understand that we all must know our weaknesses, as well as our strengths."

"So I should just give up my ambition to teach?" Monkey asked.

"I'll second that." Nick pushed himself to his feet with the cudgel.

The granny looked at Monkey, then shook her head. "Forget your own ambitions. A true teacher thinks only about what's best for his student."

Monkey stared at her for a moment, then nodded, as if he understood. Nick doubted he did.

"Come on, Salesman." Monkey motioned for Nick to follow him into the woods. "There's someone I want you to meet."

Monkey turned and headed off into the trees.

Nick followed, passing the old woman. "Thanks."

She only smiled, the twinkle in her eye reminding him a lot of the look in Kwan's eyes.

But he didn't realize that until he was almost to the edge of the meadow. When he turned back, the old woman was nowhere to be seen.

For what seemed like an eternity, Nick followed Monkey through the forest and then up a trail toward a mountain that towered over a very secluded valley to Nick's right. At one point, Nick asked Monkey how big his island really was. Monkey responded it was big enough to hold what it needed to hold.

Nick doubted they were still on the island, even though they had never crossed water. In this world in a tomb, anything was possible, as Nick was quickly learning.

Finally, after hacking their way through the deep jungle for hours, they came upon a large pagoda embedded in the side of the massive mountain. There were huge stone pillars and a curved roof barely visible through the vines and plants. It clearly had been a spectacular place in its day, covering a vast area.

"He is the greatest teacher under the Celestial Skies," Monkey said, out of the blue. "He can instruct you in the seventy-two transformations, and how to fly and somersault on clouds."

"Who is this miracle worker?" Nick stared at the ruins, which looked more like pictures of buried Mayan cities in Mexico than Chinese relics.

"His name is Patriarch Subodhi," Monkey said, "and he was my teacher."

Nick turned and looked at the Monkey King, completely shocked. "You are willing to introduce me to your own teacher?"

"Yeah. I'd like to see just how good he really is."

Monkey moved toward the ruins.

"He's in there?"

"The old place *has* gotten a little run down," Monkey said.

"You sure anyone still lives here?"

"He's a hermit," Monkey pointed out. "Where's he going to go?"

They reached the gate of what must have been the main pavilion. The ornate metal, once beautiful, had broken off its hinges and was laying on the ground, vine-covered.

"Master!" Monkey shouted into the pavilion. "Patriarch Subodhi! It is I, your most gifted student. He who has brought honor on your name and made it known before the entire world."

There was no response from the ruins.

Monkey glanced around, then shouted again. "It is Sun Wukong. The Monkey King. Four feet tall, hairy face. Remember?"

Nothing.

"Do hermits ever go on vacation?" Nick asked.

Suddenly, from somewhere in the ruins, an old-sounding voice echoed outward. "Monkey? Is that really you?"

"Yes!" Monkey brightened at the sound of his old teacher's voice. "I have come to pay my respects to my great *Shih-Fu.*"

Monkey moved forward slowly and peeked into the darkness of the ruined pavilion. Suddenly a lightning bolt flashed out, forcing Monkey to jump and roll away or be fried.

"Maybe we picked a bad time," Monkey said, standing and brushing himself off.

Nick only shrugged. It didn't surprise him that Monkey's old teacher would be angry. Nick had no doubt that most people who met Monkey soon grew angry with him.

"OK," Monkey said into the doorway, "you're upset I haven't come to visit in the past two thousand years. Is that it?"

"You wretched simian," the voice said from out of the ruin, "didn't I tell you to never show your face around here again?"

Monkey shrugged at Nick, clearly slightly embarrassed.

"Subodhi?" Nick asked.

Monkey nodded.

Subodhi went on. "Now you have the nerve to darken my gate with the stench of your disobedience?"

An old man appeared from the darkness of the ruins. The guy was a walking skeleton in rags. His clothes were old and torn, his beard long and black with filth, and he had to lean on a cane just to move.

Subodhi glared at Monkey, who for once was being silent. "Why do you think I stopped taking disciples?" The old man hobbled right up to Monkey and stared down at him in disgust. "You were the most talented pupil I had ever seen."

"At least you didn't forget that part," Monkey said.

"You wasted your precious knowledge of the Way in pursuit of selfish glory. I could have done better throwing my teachings into a pit of fire."

"Wait, wait!" Monkey held up his hand in defense as the old, thin man towered over him. "You don't get a lot of news around here, do you?"

"What use is news?" Subodhi asked. "I see only knowledge, which does not change."

"Then you haven't heard," Monkey said. "Granted, when I left here, I was still a . . ."

"An asshole?" Nick said, smiling at Monkey.

Monkey glared at Nick and then went on. "Later, after I left, I achieved great feats of virtue, and was blessed by Lord Buddha himself."

Subodhi spit in the dirt. "You're as shameless a liar today as you were the day you stepped through those gates. Everything you've done has always been for selfish reasons."

Nick stepped toward the old man. Monkey clearly needed some help, and if they were ever going to save the world above, they had to move forward right now. "Sir—"

"Who is he?" Subodhi demanded, not looking at Nick. "He carries the scent of one who has wondered too far off his path."

Nick went on, ignoring the insult, even though it hit too close to home for him to think about. "I know this may be hard to believe, but Monkey didn't bring me here today to help himself."

Subodhi turned and leered at Nick. "No?"

"He came to help me," Nick said. "Doesn't that prove he's worth another look?"

Subodhi looked Monkey up and down. Then, disgusted, he turned back toward the darkness of his ruined pavilion. "Impossible."

Nick knew at once they would need more help. He dropped to his knees and started to pray for Kwan Ying to arrive. He imagined her face, her smile, her laugh, hoping and praying she would come.

"This creature was a scoundrel," Subodhi said as he walked away. "Monkey wanted nothing more than to show off before his fellow pupils."

Nick closed his eyes, thinking as hard as he could for Kwan.

Then her voice filtered in over Subodhi's muttering. "I seem to recall another who fit that description in his youth, Honored Patriarch."

Nick opened his eyes and looked up as Kwan Ying drifted down from the sky on her cloud.

Subodhi stopped and turned around, shocked.

Kwan landed on the ground in front of Nick and smiled at him.

"Wow, this prayer stuff really works." Nick climbed to his feet.

"I was beginning to think you'd never call," Kwan said.

Subodhi fell to his knees beside her. "Kwan Ying," he said, bowing, his old bones creaking loud enough to echo in the jungle, "my favorite Bodhisattva."

"Great Immortal," Kwan said, motioning for Subodhi to stand, "this human summoned me to remind you that if you could grow from an unruly youth into your present virtue, it is possible for others to do so as well."

She looked at Monkey, then helped the struggling old man up.

"You mean he's telling the truth?" Subodhi asked.

Kwan put her hand on Monkey's shoulder. "This Great Sage traveled with the Tang priest to India, and there retrieved the sacred scriptures of Buddha."

Monkey nodded and said nothing.

"You're kidding," Subodhi said, shaking his head and pacing. After a moment he stopped and looked directly at Kwan, a light in his eyes. "So my teaching led to some good after all?"

Kwan nodded. "Virtuous words and deeds always change the world, often in ways we cannot anticipate."

Subodhi bowed to Kwan. "Forgive me for my lack of faith." He glanced up at Monkey. "Though in his case, you have to admit it was pretty understandable."

Kwan moved over and stood next to Nick. He desperately wanted to reach out and hold her hand, touch her skin again, but he managed to keep his hands at his side.

"This human has come to you for training,"

Kwan told Subodhi. "Will you do him the honor?"

Subodhi looked a little worried. "I'm a little out of practice at the Holy Master business. I mean, it's been ages."

Kwan laughed. "It's like riding a thunderbolt. You never forget how to do it, especially when you are the best."

Subodhi brightened up like he was a child given a toy. "You always were a charmer, Goddess. Think I can get you to stay for dinner?"

"Depends," Kwan said. "What's on the menu?"

"Holy words of scripture," Subodhi said. *"The Kama Sutra."*

Nick looked at Subodhi as the old man burst into laughter at his own lame joke.

Kwan had the decency to smile. "Get to work, will you? And what happened to your temple?"

Subodhi glanced around, as if seeing the overgrown mess and ruined buildings for the first time. "Oh, I've been in a bad mood, that's all."

Subodhi threw away his cane, and instantly the ruin transformed itself around them into a compound of majestic pavilions, tall red-jade towers, wonderful flowers, and arching gateways. There was even a pearl palace in the background. Subodhi himself became tall and thick, with a flowing, pure white beard.

"Wow," Nick said. "This place is really something."

"So, human." Subodhi moved over to stand in front of Nick. "What can you do? Leap across mountains? Command the seas? Call down a storm upon your enemies?"

Nick glanced at Kwan, then at Monkey. Neither of them was going to help him with this question. "Well, I've got a pretty decent backswing."

Subodhi stared at him, as if by a single look he could make Nick vanish.

All Nick could do was smile. The last time he remembered feeling that kind of stare was back in the fifth grade, when Mrs. Anderson had forced him to stand in front of the class and repeat a comment he had told to a friend in the next desk.

Finally Subodhi turned to Kwan. "This is a joke? Right?"

Kwan shook her head.

Subodhi moaned.

Nine

Nick knew the training was going to be rough. With the short lessons Monkey had tried to teach him, Nick had a hunch there were going to be some long hours and days ahead. But they didn't have days, and he wasn't sure he was up to the task of learning how to fight, no matter how long it took.

Subodhi led the entire group to a large courtyard and started Nick off by having him run with a tree limb around the paved courtyard of the pavilion. Subodhi, Monkey, and Kwan all sat in chairs in the shade, sipping drinks as he finished the first lap, carrying the limb in one hand.

As he finished, Subodhi said, "Again."

The tree limb grew, becoming heavier and thicker. Now he had to hold it with both hands.

Nick made it around the courtyard, but the second time it wasn't so easy.

Subodhi said, "Again."

The tree limb became the size of a small tree trunk, and Nick managed to stumble around once more with it before collapsing, panting, to the pavement.

"Hard," Subodhi said. "Very hard. Again."

The tree trunk grew thicker and heavier.

Nick was about to complain when he saw Kwan smile at him. Somehow, he managed to get a grip on the massive log and pull it along the pavement.

"The Way is a secret," Subodhi said, "revealed to only a few. One who reveals it to unworthy ears talks his mouth dry for no purpose."

Nick got the log around the circle and back to the point in front of his audience, then dropped it. He sat down on it and wiped his brow as Kwan smiled at him. Luckily, Subodhi had a different task for him next, because there was no chance in the world he was going to drag that thing another foot.

Subodhi moved Nick to the grass and produced a *da dao*, an ancient weapon that was nothing more than a pole with a large blade attached to one end. Nick had seen the weapon in dozens of old Chinese paintings, but never up close.

Subodhi, without a word, twirled the pole around himself, slowly gaining so much speed that he levitated off the ground.

"The world you think you know," Subodhi said, "is only an illusion."

Subodhi stopped his demonstration and tossed the pole to Nick. The thing was heavy and awkward, and Nick barely managed not to drop it.

"A mirror image of the true world, which you have forgotten existed at all."

Nick looked at Subodhi, who was making no

sense at all with his stupid sayings. The guy was one-liner after one-liner. Monkey was smiling. Kwan just looked at him with encouragement.

"Defend," Subodhi said, moving away and leaving a completely see-through outline of his shape.

"Against what?" Nick asked.

"Your invisible partner." Monkey pointed at the projection.

As Nick stared at the vague outlines of the almost invisible Subodhi, the image threw a bolt of energy. It hit him squarely in the chest, knocking him back as if someone had punched him, and it hurt like hell. The thing tossing those bolts might be almost nonexistent, but the bolts were very real.

"Defend with the *da dao*."

The see-through projection of Subodhi reared back and threw another bolt of energy. Nick tried to block it with the blade and missed. The energy bolt almost knocked the wind out of him as it smashed into his stomach.

"Travel with me there," the real Subodhi said, "and the reality of your life will finally be revealed."

The next energy bolt caught Nick in the chin and sent him tumbling over backward in the grass.

He pushed himself to his feet. He was bruised, cut, exhausted, and angry. "I'm not taking any more of this crap! Enough is enough."

He kicked the *da dao* away and turned and headed into the orchard. What had made him think he could ever be anything more than a businessman? This was the stupidest thing he had ever done.

He walked far enough into the peach orchard to feel alone, then sat down, his back against the bark of a tree. He was not going to kill himself trying to please people who were myths.

"Are you all right?" Kwan's voice asked, concern in her soft tone.

"Who the hell do you all think I am?" he asked, not looking up at her. "Bruce Lee?"

She laughed and sat down beside him.

"This ain't exactly like a game of racquetball," he said. "And the old man's gobbledygook—I've heard that crap before on late-night cable from new-age nutcases."

Kwan picked up a smashed peach and held it in her hand so he could see it. "Yes, this is all impossible. I know."

As she spoke the peach seemed to shrink, growing younger and younger, until it turned into a beautiful blossom. "But all the most wonderful things are."

She offered him the blossom and he took it, careful to not smash it.

"It has a wonderful scent," she said.

He sniffed the flower. Instantly his cuts, aches, and bruises went away. He felt as if he'd had a full night's sleep, more refreshed than he had been in a long, long time.

He turned so he could face her. "You know, I've never met a woman who was literally an angel."

Kwan touched his arm and leaned in close.

"Tell you a secret. Don't catch me on a bad day. No woman is an angel *all* the time."

Nick laughed. His anger was gone.

She touched his arm lightly, her skin soft and warm against his. "There's no limit to what you can do, Nick."

He wanted to lean over and kiss her. She had called him by his nickname. And she believed in him. What more could any man want or need?

"All right." He pushed himself to his feet. "Let's go show that invisible guy with the energy bolts a thing or two."

She laughed and walked with him back to the open grass area. Subodhi and Monkey were sitting at a table, staring off in opposite directions, clearly not talking to each other. Kwan moved over to join them as Nick picked up the *da dao*. For some reason it felt more natural in his hands, not at all alien and out of balance as it had a short time ago.

The outline of the invisible partner moved to toss another bolt. Nick swung the blade like a racquet, hitting the bolt and smashing it back into the invisible partner. The creature vanished in a puff of smoke.

Kwan applauded. Even Monkey looked impressed.

Subodhi stood and motioned for Nick to follow him through the estate to the edge of a massive cliff. Far, far below, clouds and mist drifted over rocks. What looked like a river wound down the valley, but it was so far below that the water was no more than a thin blue thread among the green and brown.

Subodhi took Nick by the hand and moved him to the edge of the cliff. "Concentrate," the old man said. He picked up Nick in hands much stronger than they appeared, and sat him down so that his right foot was hanging out over thin air. His left foot was planted firmly on the cliff.

"Are you nuts?" Nick shouted.

"Concentrate or fall," Subodhi said. "Your choice. Always."

The old man let go.

Somehow Nick managed to stay balanced on his left foot, his right foot dangling over a thousand-foot drop.

"Good." Subodhi turned and walked away. Monkey, without a word, followed him.

Kwan sat down on the grass, put her legs into a lotus position, and seemed to go into a trance.

Nick could feel his left leg already starting to buckle. If he stayed focused on balancing, he could stay centered over the leg, taking the pressure off of it. And staying centered over his left leg took less energy.

He took slow, deep breaths and focused on the balance. If Kwan thought he could do this, if she thought he could do anything, then he would show her she was right.

Slowly the sun sat.

Kwan did not move.

Nick did not move. He didn't dare. He concentrated on staying balanced, not looking either up or down or sideways. Simply being.

And the more he concentrated, the more at peace he became there on that cliff top.

"Be not afraid." Kwan's voice drifted into his mind like a soft breeze, gentle and warm. "Be not afraid to open your heart."

Slowly the cliff vanished from Nick's mind, the need to stay centered, balanced.

He moved inside himself, walked along in his own mind, no longer on that cliff. And then he was to that *one* point when everything in his life had changed, the one point that seemed to be the center of who he had become.

He was back in Chicago, in his apartment in college. Back when he was still studying Chinese history.

"I'm sorry, Nick," Linda said. "I'm so sorry."

The woman of his heart, his every waking moment for the past three years, sat on their bed, her head bowed. Her long brown hair covered her face; her thin hands locked together in her lap. She wore a thick coat, jeans, and snow boots. Nick paced in front of her, trying to make sense of what was happening to him. But his mind just wasn't accepting it.

"I'm so sorry," she repeated.

"But I love you," Nick said. "And you love me. Since when is that not enough?"

"I can't explain." She looked up at him with the brown eyes he had spent years looking into. "Paul is different."

"He's your boss."

Nick knew Paul, Linda's boss in the history department. He had taken classes from Paul. So had Linda before going to work for him part-time as a graduate assistant.

Linda pushed herself to her feet. "I'm sorry. I've got to go."

"That's it?" Nick asked, his anger and panic boiling over. "Don't I even deserve an explanation?"

Linda, tears filling her eyes, just stared at him. Then she turned and bolted for the door, her steps like gunshots on the staircase.

Nick waited until the front door of the apartment building slammed closed, then moved to the window. Linda ran down the front walk and into the arms of Paul, who led her to his car, which was parked down the block.

Nick watched until they were gone, then turned and looked at his apartment, at the table where the two of them had studied so long and hard. The Chinese print on the wall was like a knife cutting into his stomach. He could never return to that history department. Ever.

He moved to the wall and calmly ripped the print down.

And as he did, he found himself back, standing balanced over the edge of the cliff. His leg felt like lead, his body was trembling, he had lost his center focus, and he felt as if he might fall at any moment. He closed his eyes, trying to concentrate, but the memories were like water flooding a room, impossible to hold back.

"I can't go on," he said, softly. The memory of Linda, of what he had given up that day, was a fresh dagger in his stomach.

Suddenly there was the feeling of soft silk on his cheek. He opened his eyes to see Kwan sitting on her cloud beside him.

"Only the bravest among us are willing to

face their past," she said. "I am so proud of
you."

Nick leaned his head gently against her, his
strength again back in his body, his concentra-
tion clear. At that moment, he knew he could
stand there on that cliff face, centered and balanced, for as long as he needed to.

Ten

Nick could not remember ever living a day like the one he had gone through, and it showed no signs of ending anytime soon. For the last three hours in lantern light, he had practiced twirling the *da dao,* as Subodhi had taught him to do. He wasn't anywhere near close to getting it right. He either dropped it or hit himself with it.

Subodhi and Monkey had long ago disappeared into another part of the pavilion, leaving Nick to his practicing. Kwan was asleep on a carved ebony bench.

What he really wanted to do was have this mastered by the time she woke up. He took the heavy stick with the blade on the end and spun it in front of him, like a twirler would spin a baton in front of a band in a parade. Then he tried to move the *da dao* behind his back. His grip slipped, and he ducked his head as the flat side of the metal blade came around and slapped him on the cheek.

"I'm too old for this." He kept his voice soft so as to not wake Kwan. He gazed at her sleeping form.

Kwan had to be more beautiful in sleep than awake, if that was possible. In all his life he could not remember being so attracted to another person. As he stared at her, he remembered her words.

Be not afraid to open your heart.

He stepped closer to her and softly said, "It's been a long time since I met a girl I could see spending the rest of my life with. Just my luck it should be you."

He looked at her, his every sense wanting to touch her, to comfort her, to be with her. "Goddess, I love you."

Suddenly, the *da dao* in his hand came to life. For an instant he wanted to resist, not believing. Then he cleared his mind, as he had learned to do on the cliff face, and found his balance. He let the weapon guide him, let his muscles flow, making its every movement his movement.

The *da dao* put Nick through a breathtaking exhibition of twirls, spins, jabs, and swipes. It was as if Subodhi himself was inside his arms and the weapon.

"Kwan!" Nick shouted as he learned, gaining control, moving with an agility he never knew he had. Yet now, somehow, that agility felt natural and right.

Kwan opened her eyes, and Nick let himself go even faster and faster, becoming completely one with the weapon.

The *da dao* was a blur around him. He could feel himself getting lighter and lighter. He loved the feeling, memorized it, made it a part of himself.

And then, as he did, he lifted off the ground, the *da dao* a vision of motion around him. He moved himself at first ten, then twenty feet off the ground, easing backward, forward, testing, never missing a movement.

Then he lowered himself down to a position right in front of the wide-eyed Kwan and stopped, his heart racing, every fiber in his being knowing he could do the same thing again at any moment.

"Did you see that?" Nick asked Kwan. "That was awesome."

"You were awesome." Kwan stepped forward and gave him a hug he would never forget. It was as if every curve in her body fit perfectly with every curve in his. Her arms fit with his, her strength flowed with his.

Even their breathing matched.

He pulled his head back just enough so he could look into her eyes without letting go, without moving away from the full-body embrace.

And in her eyes he saw what he knew was also in his eyes—love, desire, and a depth of understanding he hadn't realized was possible.

He moved his head forward until his lips touched hers.

In the background he swore he heard a thousand choirs backed by a thousand orchestras spring into being as her lips pushed into his.

Her passion matched his.

The moment became a lifetime.

"Scholar?" Subodhi asked, his voice like a distant bell, gaining power and awareness, pushing between them like a cold hand. "Goddess?"

It was as if someone had flicked off the music. Nick stepped back from Kwan as she stepped back from him. He was suddenly only half of what he had been a moment before.

Kwan's face was red, her eyes downcast as she turned to Monkey and Subodhi. "He flew!" she said.

She reached over and took his hand, holding it aloft like he was a champion. "He actually flew!"

Both Subodhi and Monkey just stared as Nick took a deep bow, never wanting to let go of Kwan's hand.

An hour later, after Nick had demonstrated his new ability with the *da dao* and flight, the four of them were standing in the courtyard as Monkey and Subodhi argued. Nick wasn't listening to what they were saying. His focus was on Kwan and finding a way to spend more time alone with her.

"A few seconds off the ground," Subodhi said to Monkey, "and you think he's ready to fight armies."

"We haven't got time for perfection," Monkey replied, standing down his old teacher. "We can spend the night in Tuoluo Village and reach the Masters' hideout tomorrow."

Subodhi snorted, then turned to Kwan. "Will you please talk some sense into this creature?"

Kwan pulled her gaze from Nick and looked

at the old Subodhi. Then she straightened her shoulders and turned squarely back to face Nick. "Do you feel you are ready to continue the pilgrimage?"

Nick knew the answer to the question was important, but he wasn't sure exactly why. He did understand that there was little time, and he had come to believe in his heart that his world was in danger.

"Goddess," he said, "I feel like I'm ready for anything."

Kwan looked at him, frustrated, but accepting his answer. Around her feet a cloud appeared and lifted her toward the sky. "Then you must go."

She stared at Nick as he raised his hand for her to stay. He hadn't intended to push her away. That had been the last thing he wanted to do. Then he remembered her words, that she would be with him always, and all he had to do was pray for her.

An instant later, she disappeared in a flash of light.

Subodhi shook his head. "Great. There goes my reason to keep the place looking pretty."

Around them the compound transformed back into the old ruins and overgrown jungle.

Subodhi picked up his old cane and looked at Monkey. "Once again you have disappointed me." He turned and started into the ruined pavilion.

"No," Monkey said. "Once again, Master, I have learned from you."

Subodhi stopped and looked back at Monkey. "That sounded almost humble."

"You have shown me what it means to be a real teacher," Monkey said.

The two looked at each other until finally Nick decided they needed to get going. "Patriarch Subodhi, may we have your blessing?"

Monkey and Nick both saluted Subodhi in the traditional Chinese show of respect.

Subodhi snorted. "Foolish human. Who cares about a blessing? What you need is a weapon."

Beside Nick, Monkey jerked as if slapped.

Subodhi shook his head and stared at Monkey. "That little detail slip your mind, did it? Some warrior you are. Forget to get a weapon. Now get out of here and find one."

Monkey laughed. "Master, it was good to see you again after all these years."

Subodhi nodded. "Come again sometime, will you? It is rare I get the opportunity to laugh."

Slowly, Subodhi brought his hands together and bowed slightly, saluting them. Nick had never felt so honored in his entire life.

Monkey grabbed Nick's arm and leaped into the sky. Unlike the first time, Nick was comfortable in the flight, not at all afraid or worried.

Behind them Nick heard Subodhi shout to him, "Don't forget to keep balancing on one leg. All night, every night."

Monkey's jump took them far above the land and out over the open sea, peaking at a point that seemed against the top of the sky. Below them was nothing but the deep blue of open ocean.

"Where are we going?" Nick scanned below for a rock or island as they started down. There was nothing but water.

"Where does it look like?" Monkey asked.

"In case you've forgotten," Nick pointed out as the waves got closer and closer, "humans can't breathe under water."

"Details, details." Monkey moved his hand over Nick just as they hit the water.

Nick held his breath as long as he could as they went deeper and deeper. Finally, making sure he was holding on to Monkey's hand tight just in case, he opened his mouth and took a mouthful of water. Only it wasn't water. Somehow it was air.

"What did you do?" Nick asked, his voice sounding hollow in the water.

"I've waterproofed your fur." Monkey shrugged. "Plus a few other things."

Nick decided to not ask any more questions. Below them, lit as if the sun was shining directly on it, he could see a pagoda-topped palace sprawling over the ocean floor. It was surrounded by waves of coral, tall columns that looked like octopus arms, and portals shaped like the open mouths of fish.

"This is the palace of the Dragon King," Monkey said.

Monkey and Nick landed, bounced, and then sort of floated near the gate as two octopus guards scrambled inside, clearly afraid.

"No one to welcome me?" Monkey asked, looking around.

"It's not exactly like we called ahead," Nick said, his voice sounding more and more normal in the water.

Monkey led the way through the majestic gates, half walking, half swimming. Nick managed to keep up and stare at the same time at the fantastic giant statues of sea creatures that lined the main corridor.

"Kind of makes you hungry for seafood, doesn't it?" Monkey asked, pointing to one statue.

At the other end of the corridor a large, serpentine lizard-like creature appeared. Scales flowed from its head down its back to its feet. Nick figured this had to be the Dragon King.

The King frantically tried to pull on a royal red robe as he swam toward Monkey and Nick. A dozen octopus advisers floated along behind him, clearly agitated. Finally, getting the robe fastened, the King reached them. "Brother Monkey. No one told us you were coming."

Monkey said nothing.

"Tell me," the King said, "how is the great gold-banded cudgel which you so graciously removed from our armory?"

Nick glanced at Monkey and then back at the Dragon King. It was clear this was not a friendly relationship, but one that Monkey had the complete upper hand in.

Monkey took the tiny cudgel from behind his ear and held it up. "Good as new. Would you like to see it grow to full size?"

The Dragon King almost passed out at that idea. His octopus advisers all moved back closer to the walls, flailing their arms.

"No! No!" the King said. "It would break through the walls of our palace." The King moved past Nick and Monkey toward the front door. "So if there's nothing else we can do for you—"

Nick wanted to laugh, but instead kept his poker face. Clearly Monkey was the very last person they wanted to have visit.

"My friend needs a weapon," Monkey said. "Don't worry. I can find my way to the armory."

"But they are *our* weapons," the Dragon King said.

Monkey ignored the comment, pulling Nick along to a massive underwater cavern beneath the palace, which was filled with thousands of different types of weapons. The King and his advisers followed a distance behind.

"Impressive collection, isn't it?" Monkey moved inside and tried the first weapon he came to, breaking it almost instantly. He held the remains of the weapon up to Nick. "Cheap. Shattered like glass. Don't worry, Scholar. I'll find you a weapon if I have to reduce the entire collection to rubble."

Behind him Nick heard the King sob.

Monkey moved along the rows of weapons, occasionally trying one and breaking it, then tossing it aside and trying another. Finally Monkey dug down into a small pile of odd-looking weapons and pulled out a *mao-pi*.

A *mao-pi* was a brush-pen used for Chinese

calligraphy. Nick had no idea what it was doing in a collection of weapons. But clearly Monkey had other thoughts.

"Ah." Monkey held the pen up and looked at it. "Here is a mighty tool of war, perfectly suited to your talents."

"It's a brush," Nick said.

"A scholar's writing brush."

Nick shook his head. "What am I supposed to do with it? Tickle their noses and hope they sneeze to death?"

To one side Nick could see the Dragon King give him a thumbs up, encouraging him to take the pen as his choice.

"Master," Monkey said, "think of my comrades from *Journey to the West*. With a cudgel, a rake, and the staff of a priest, we defeated the demons of hell. It is not the weapon which matters, but the spirit of the fighter who uses it."

The Dragon King nodded so hard he caused currents around himself.

Nick reached out and took the small brush from Monkey.

"Grow," Monkey said.

The brush turned into a staff about five feet long, solid in Nick's hands. Maybe Monkey was right. He swung the brush around as he had done with the *da dao*. Even under the water he could move it with such grace and speed that it became almost invisible in his hands, lifting him from the bottom.

"Here is a warrior whose coming Buddha foretold," Monkey said, gesturing to Nick. "The Scholar From Above."

Around them the Dragon King and his advisers burst into cheers. Nick had no doubt that the cheers were not for him, but for the fact that he and Monkey would be leaving soon.

And not breaking any more weapons.

Eleven

Far above the ocean where Nick and Monkey were getting Nick's new weapon, the Jade Emperor's palace floated atop the white clouds of heaven. It was an enormous place, enclosed by walls surrounding buildings and courtyards as vast as the old Forbidden City.

In massive, gold-lined halls and lush chambers, gods devoted themselves to pleasure. Wonderful music floated in the air no matter where anyone went, and there was happiness everywhere—except when Confucius turned his attention on a person. No one liked him, but all feared him and his position of power with the Emperor. He was the ultimate wet blanket in a world full of sunshine.

Kwan Ying's feelings toward Confucius were no exception. Being called to Confucius's office in the Palace of Heavenly Purity was like being called to the headmaster's office in school.

With this summons, Kwan knew there were going to be problems. She just didn't know what they would be. So she had Whitesnake, her assistant, a woman who wore a white snake's body, go with her for support and to make sure she didn't miss something important.

Confucius's secretary, a gnome-like creature as ugly as they came, led Kwan and Whitesnake into the stark, dark office, then stood beside the old man's desk. Confucius, his white beard making his rail-thin face seem even longer, continued to flip through papers, forcing Kwan and Whitesnake to stand and wait until he was finished. Kwan hated that old trick, but with Confucius, she had to admit it worked.

Finally, he looked up at them.

"Lord Confucius," Kwan said, "you called for me."

He nodded. "We have learned that Monkey is on his way to retrieve *Journey to the West* from the Masters. I want to know if he plans to act quickly."

Kwan was stunned. How in the heavens had Confucius heard so soon what was happening? What more did he know about?

"The Prime Minister has asked you a question!" Confucius's secretary barked. "Do not forget he speaks for the Jade Emperor."

Kwan gave the old gnome a dirty look, as if anyone could ever forget where Confucius got his power, and then answered the question. "Yes, Monkey is arriving even tonight in Tuoluo Village, but—"

"That's all I need to know." Confucius waved her away.

Kwan nodded and turned to leave, Whitesnake at her side. Then she decided she had to have an answer. "How did you find out?"

she asked, turning back to face Confucius. "Does the Jade Emperor support our efforts?"

"The Prime Minister has dismissed you," the secretary said.

Confucius waved aside the gnome. "His Highness, the Jade Emperor, has taken a strict position of neutrality. He feels the author of the book, Author Wu, has the authority to determine where it belongs."

"But Author Wu disappeared centuries ago," Kwan said. "No one can find him. Surely you must understand the suffering that would befall humans above if they are suddenly forced to live as their ancestors did five hundred years ago."

"Five hundred years ago?" Confucius asked, smiling at her with black teeth. "When China was the world's greatest power? Not everyone here believes that would be such a bad thing."

Confucius and his secretary smiled at each other, clearly sharing the belief between them. Kwan was appalled by the very idea that saving the world above did not have full support in the Jade Palace.

"All we ask," Confucius said, looking at Kwan directly, "is that this dispute be settled quickly. If it drags on, the ensuing controversy may cause chaos and division in our world. In other words, the sooner the human leaves here, the better."

Kwan instantly didn't like what the Prime Minister had said. "He survived the booby traps," she said. "He has every right to remain.

If you try to remove him, I'll complain to the Jade Emperor Himself."

Confucius looked at her, studied her for a moment, then smiled. "Did I say anything about removing him?"

Kwan didn't change her stance or her posture, but she knew she had betrayed too much information about her feelings for Nick.

"Goddess," Confucius said, "you must work toward achieving inner peace."

With that he waved her away and she turned, glad to be away from the old goat.

In silence, she and Whitesnake moved out into the open courtyard and started through the trees toward her chambers. The sun felt good on her back, calming her some. She turned to Whitesnake. "I hate it when I lose my serenity in front of that oaf."

Whitesnake cleared her throat. "Mistress, I hate to say it, but Confucius has a point. The way you speak of that human, the look in your eyes . . ."

Kwan continued walking, keeping her gaze ahead. She was stunned that her feelings for Nick were that obvious.

"I fear you are becoming personally involved."

"That's absurd," Kwan said, trying to brush away the comments she knew in her heart were true.

"Remember what happened to Bodhisattva Chen Jung?"

The name rang a bell, but not a clear one. "Who?"

"Chen Jung," Whitesnake repeated. "She fell in love with the human she was watching over. What was his name? Bald, short, wore glasses?"

"Gandhi?"

"Right," Whitesnake said. "And once she lost her love for her work, she also lost her powers."

Kwan did remember that now, and the memory sobered her. "Thank you for your concern."

But Whitesnake was not going to let it go so easily. "I want you to swear you will work to master your emotions."

"Don't be ridiculous." Kwan stared at her assistant. "You're treating me like a novice."

"If you are not in love," Whitesnake said, "you shouldn't be afraid to swear."

Kwan couldn't let this assistant get the better of her. She placed her palms together. "I swear I will work to master my emotions."

"Great," Whitesnake said, happy with what Kwan had done. "Just don't forget that beings fall in love with *you*. You do not fall in love with *them*."

Kwan said nothing as the clear image of Nick came to her mind. It was as if he were there with her. She could feel the wonderful passion of his kiss, the sound of his laughter, the desire in his skin. Her feelings were real. She knew that. But for Nick's sake, and the entire world above, she had to be careful. She had to do as she promised and master her emotions.

With Monkey holding Nick's arm, they burst into the late afternoon sky, flashing toward

Tuoluo Village. To Nick it felt great to be out of the ocean and back in the air, even though his clothes were not wet and he could breathe just fine underwater. It hadn't felt natural at all. The air was where he belonged.

Monkey landed them on a slight ridge just out of sight of the village and immediately turned toward the top. "I once saved this village from a demon," Monkey said. "They'll welcome us and let me rest while you practice all night."

"Sounds wonderful," Nick said as sarcastically as he could.

At that moment they cleared the top of the ridge. Spread out before them were the smoking remains of what had been a beautiful place.

"Dear Buddha." Monkey ran forward.

Nick followed, looking around. The damage was still fresh, that much was for sure. Fires were burning in huts, and bodies were strewn around the open square in the center. The place smelled of sulfur and death.

"Old Liang!" Monkey shouted and stopped beside a man kneeling over a body. "Old Liang, it's me, the Great Sage Monkey. What happened here?"

Nick joined Monkey as the old man looked up, tears of rage filling his eyes. "You gods," Liang said, his voice cold and angry. "You treat us like your toys."

He slumped to the ground and held the hand of the dead woman, who must have been his wife. The old man looked at Monkey, then at Nick. "Could you ever know what it means to lose the woman you love?"

Nick bent down and put his arm on the old man's shoulders. "We need to know what happened," Nick said as gently as he could.

"A demon from the high mountains attacked the village for no reason at all. What did we do to deserve this?"

Nick felt the man shudder as sobs wracked his body. He held the old man for a moment as around them the village burned in the late afternoon sun.

Finally Monkey broke the silence. "Tell us where the creature came from, and we'll—"

"—kick some demon butt." Nick finished Monkey's sentence.

Two minutes later they were headed out of the ruins of the village and into the mountains. All Nick wanted to do was avenge the people there. He had a sneaking hunch they had died because someone knew he and Monkey were headed there. And if Nick could kill a demon, it would sure make him feel better.

It took them another hour, until just after nightfall, before they found the exact area the old man had told them about. It was a rock-covered slope on a mountain. Nick was leading the way up the steep incline, going as fast as he could over the rocks and rough dirt.

"Slow down," Monkey said from behind him. "You don't know when the demon might strike."

"Stop worrying." Nick patted the brush-pen tucked into his belt.

"You're not that good yet."

"I'm good enough." Nick climbed over more rocks. "You told Patriarch Subodhi yourself."

"I was exaggerating," Monkey said. "For one thing, you could stand some work on the sin of pride."

"Oh," Nick said, smiling back at Monkey, "look who's talking."

"It's not pride when you really *are* a genius."

"Well, Kwan Ying thinks I'm pretty great, too." The image of Kwan had never been far from his mind since she had left them.

Suddenly Monkey shouted, "Behind you!"

Nick whirled around to come face to face with a giant serpent. The thing was bigger than a train and had a set of teeth that could crush a house.

Monkey had his cudgel out as Nick dived past him, barely avoiding the monster jaws and the razor-sharp teeth of the serpent. The serpent, angry at missing Nick, whipped out its long forked tongue and wrapped it around Monkey's cudgel, yanking Monkey into the air in a massive tug-of-war.

Nick stopped and turned to watch, his brush now five feet long in his hand. Monkey gave his own weapon a mighty tug, almost yanking the tongue right out of the head of the serpent.

Then, right next to Nick, another boulder moved.

And opened its eyes.

And then its mighty jaws.

There were two serpents. This had been a trap!

"Monkey!" Nick screamed.

The second serpent's tongue wrapped around Nick as he beat at it with his brush, using every move he could remember from his training. Above him, in the air, Monkey was riding the second demon like a bronco. He was going to be no help at the moment.

The tongue was rough and stronger than anything Nick could have imagined. It pulled him slowly but surely toward the open mouth, the razor-sharp teeth, and the dripping milky venom.

Nick, thinking as fast as he could, twisted and jumped up on the base of the serpent's tongue, riding it over the lower teeth like a surf board over a wave.

Then, just as the jaws were about to bite down on him, he turned his brush upward, jamming it into the roof of the serpent's mouth.

It stopped the jaws from closing.

Enraged, the serpent flailed about, doing its best to dislodge the stick. Foul air rushed up out of the serpent, carrying with it the smell of death and rotted fish.

Nick held on to his brush as he was whipped from side to side in the demon's mouth. He wasn't sure how long he could hold on, but somehow he had to.

Around him rotting body parts of humans stuck in the teeth, left over from the attack on the village. A dense, blackish fog oozed from the decaying gums. Between the half-eaten human flesh and the rotting gums, the smell was choking Nick. If the demon didn't kill him, the bad breath would.

Again the monster shook its head from side to side, trying to dislodge the brush and smashing Nick around in the process. Finally, on a calm moment, Nick decided he couldn't take much more of that. He was going to have to do some fighting.

He grabbed the brush and yanked it from the roof of the serpent's mouth. As the creature stopped moving, surprised, Nick jammed the brush into its worst-looking dental cavity.

"Check-up time!" Nick shouted.

The serpent let out a bellow more intense than a hundred lightning bolts. Then it darted into the sky beside the demon Monkey was fighting.

"A little help!" Nick shouted out of the demon's open mouth at Monkey as the two demons passed in the air.

Monkey apparently had not even noticed the serpent that had Nick until that very moment. His face grew red and angry. "The left hand make fog, so the right hand may strike! I hate that technique!"

With one mighty blow of his cudgel, Monkey cut the first serpent's head from its body.

Nick wanted to cheer, but then realized the serpent he was riding in was about to bite down on him again.

He jammed the brush into its gums, and again the beast let out a mighty roar. But the thrashing of the second attack made Nick lose his grip on the brush.

And the slimy surface of the demon's tongue was too slick to get a good hold on.

He went down and headed feet first into the darkness of the demon's gullet. His brush stuck in the gum, holding the demon's mouth open and shoving the brush deeper into the painful cavity every time it tried to close.

"Grab hold!" Nick heard Monkey shout from above as a rope slid past him.

Nick twisted his body in midair and grabbed the safety line as Monkey joined him, hanging above the pit of steaming acid that was the monster's stomach. The smell choked Nick, and the sight of half-digested human bodies made him sick.

"Hope those tonsils hold." Monkey looked down at the acid. Back up the throat, Nick could see Monkey had tied the hair rope around the demon's tonsils.

"Time for some fresh air," Monkey said.

With a mighty whack from his cudgel, he cut a square opening in the side of the creature. Then, grabbing Nick by the arm, Monkey leaped through the opening and into the fresh air of the sky. A jet of steam propelled them away from the serpent as it slashed through the night like a balloon losing its air.

Monkey landed them on the side of the mountain and they watched as the second serpent flip-flopped through the skies.

"Rule number one," Monkey said. "When fighting demons, I go first. Understand?"

"OK," Nick said, "so I made a mistake."

"Because of your mistake, I almost made a mistake as well."

Thomas Gibson is Nick Orton

Russell Wong is The Monkey King

Nick trains for the battle of his life

Eddie Marsan is Pigsy

Kabir Bedi is Friar Sand

Bai Ling is Kwan Ying

Monkey, Nick, Pigsy and Friar Sand: a motley group of heroes

The famed Chinese god: The Monkey King

Monkey, Kwan Ying and Nick join forces
to protect the future of the world

The beautiful goddess, Kwan Ying

The Monkey King prepares for battle

Nick readies for the challenge of his life

Beautiful and mysterious Kwan Ying

The emperor's bloody campaign to destroy the manuscript of
<u>Journey to the West</u>

Supporters rally to the cause of The Monkey King

The determined adversaries...

A forbidden romance

Kwan Ying, Pigsy and Friar Sand—the magical heroes of the Monkey King

A love that spans two worlds

The ground shook as the second serpent smashed into the rocks.

"The Masters must know we're coming," Monkey said. "That trap was meant for you."

"I know." The thought of all the people killed in the village made Nick both sober and angry.

Below their feet, the ground continued to rumble. Nick looked off at the corpse of the second serpent, his brush poking out of the top of its mouth. The demon was clearly dead.

"Why is the ground still shaking?" Monkey asked.

Nick looked behind them. The mountain was collapsing.

"Could that be the reason?" Nick pointed upward.

Monkey turned, took one look, grabbed Nick's arm, and jumped, getting out of the way as the mountain was quickly reduced to a pile of rubble and a dense cloud of dust.

Monkey and Nick landed on some rocks, staring at where the mountain had been a few minutes ago. Suddenly two figures appeared in the dust, brushing off their clothes and coughing.

"Holy Buddha," one figure said, "I'm starving. Do you think we can find a place that will let us eat before we wash up?"

"Pigsy?" Monkey said. "Is that you?"

Nick looked at Monkey, his mind not believing what Monkey was saying, then back at the two figures, who were now completely out of the dust. Nick couldn't believe it. There stood a pig on his hind legs. He was about four feet tall and carried a rake. The other figure was a massive behemoth garbed in the brown robes of a wandering priest. He carried a staff and wore a necklace of human skulls.

Exactly how the old Chinese prints pictured them. Only dirtier.

"Pigsy and Friar Sand," Nick said as Monkey rushed toward his old friends, "from *Journey to the West.*"

Twelve

Nick was so stunned he couldn't even speak as the friends of legend, the two who had roamed with Monkey in the famous book *Journey to the West*, reunited again. Watching it happen was like being a kid watching real comic book characters come to life. Nick had read the book so many times, studied it over and over. Now he was meeting everyone who had been in it. Stunned was the only way to describe how he felt.

They headed down the mountain, talking about old times, and ended up in a grove of persimmons, where Pigsy picked and devoured as much fruit as he could reach or knock down with his rake.

"When you killed those serpent demons," the Friar said, "it broke the spell on the mountain where the Masters had imprisoned us."

Monkey nodded. "So Shu also made certain you could not threaten him."

"It would seem that way," the Friar said. "Or rescue you."

"Who is this human with you?" Pigsy asked. "And does he like persimmons?"

Nick declined the persimmon Pigsy offered, much to the pig's delight. Until that moment, Nick had not realized he had not been introduced to the Friar and Pigsy. He knew them from the legends and stories, but they didn't know him.

"He is a very important scholar," Monkey said.

Both Friar and Pigsy looked at Nick.

"He doesn't look like a scholar," the Friar said.

"Never fear," Monkey said, "I am his teacher."

Pigsy spit out a persimmon and burst into choking laughter. Monkey stared at him.

Finally Pigsy managed to say, "You and who else?"

"You are supposed to be my comrades." Monkey was clearly angry at Pigsy's laughter.

"Yes," Friar said, "that is why we can tell you the truth."

Nick knew at once it was the wrong thing to say. Monkey picked the cudgel from behind his ear and it grew in his hands.

The Friar kicked his staff up into his hands.

Pigsy picked up his rake. The three heroes of the famous book stood facing each other, weapons ready.

"What do you know anyway?" Monkey said to Pigsy. "You never even achieved Buddhahood."

"I could have if I'd only been able to control my appetite, which I will start to do as soon as I finish eating."

"Gods, gods," Nick said, stepping toward them. "Settle down. Do you always get along this well?"

Embarrassed, Monkey lowered his weapon. The other two did the same.

"The scholar is right," Monkey said. "The truth is we must all work together. Kwan Ying has sent me on a very important pilgrimage."

Friar Sand and Pigsy both took a step toward Monkey at the sound of Kwan's name.

"Kwan Ying." Pigsy drooled more at saying the words than he had eating the persimmons. "If we come, will she join us? Maybe even spend a few days?"

"Excuse me." Nick stepped into the group. "Is everyone down here in love with Kwan Ying?"

They all turned and stared at him as if he'd just asked if the sky was blue and clouds were white.

Finally Monkey turned to the rest of them. "We are going to rescue the original manuscript of *Journey to the West* from the Masters."

"Then the Scholar From Above has come at last," Pigsy said. "Where is he?"

Monkey nodded toward Nick.

Nick smiled, but the look on both Pigsy's face and the extra frown on the Friar's face told him he wasn't their top choice.

"I think you need our help," Friar said.

Pigsy nodded, biting into another persimmon.

Nick could tell that Monkey was excited for the first time on this trip. "With the three of us heroes reunited, can anyone in creation doubt we will succeed?"

Friar stepped forward and faced Nick and Monkey. "I pledge my allegiance."

Monkey glanced around to where Pigsy had moved off a few steps, eating. "Pigsy, are you with us?"

Pigsy looked up, his face covered with the red pulp of the fruit. "Oh, sure. Count me in."

Nick practiced his exercises for a few hours and then napped. When he awoke, the sun was coming up, but Monkey was still sleeping. Pigsy and Friar were sitting on a slight ridge, watching the sunrise splash reds and oranges across the sky.

As Nick approached, Friar said, "Just like I remembered it." He glanced up at Nick. "When you are imprisoned, it is the simple things you miss the most. A sunrise."

Nick glanced up at the beauty of it. There didn't seem to be a setting in this world that wasn't beautiful. It was amazing so many ugly things went on inside such beauty.

"Fresh air." Nick took a deep breath.

"Breakfast," Pigsy said. "Hot eggs."

"Sizzling bacon," Nick said, remembering the smell of his mother's kitchen.

Pigsy turned and glared at him until Nick realized what he had said. "Oh, sorry."

"Lacking such things," Friar said, "at times I wish they had just killed me."

Nick stared at the Friar, not really believing

what he had just heard. They were already in heaven, weren't they? "Is it possible in this world for you to die?"

"Yes," the Friar said. "Our life force can be returned to the cosmos. Of course, it is extremely difficult to take the *chi* from gods like us."

Pigsy motioned at Monkey. "And hardest of all from him. Believe it or not, his *chi* is bigger than his head."

Nick and Pigsy both laughed, but Friar just stared at them.

"It's a joke," Pigsy said, disgusted with the Friar. "A joke." Pigsy turned to Nick. "Imagine, a guy as funny as I am, imprisoned for centuries with someone who has no sense of humor."

Nick just stared at Friar, who said nothing and didn't seem to notice the insult.

"Monkey's going to be up soon," Pigsy said. "I'd better forage for breakfast." He headed off into the woods, leaving Nick alone with Friar.

"He's not that funny," Nick said to Friar, trying to ease the sting of the insult.

"Brother Pig is correct," Friar said. "I am a great warrior. I have even achieved Buddhahood. And yet I do not know how to laugh."

Friar looked at Nick, then stepped closer as if to make sure no one else heard his question. "Are you funny?"

"We are all funny sometimes," Nick said. "Even you. When you looked at me and said, *I think you need our help*, that was funny."

"But I was being sincere," Friar said, puzzled.

Nick patted the huge man's arm. "We'll work on it."

Sand looked at Nick, a glimmer of excitement in his eyes. "Then you will be my teacher?" The monster Friar turned and dropped to his knees in front of Nick, bowing. "Great *Shih-Fu*, I thank you for your faith and trust."

Nick was so embarrassed he didn't know what to do. Down the hill he could see Monkey starting to stir. He pulled the Friar up to his feet before Monkey could see what was going on.

A moment later Monkey sprang to his feet. "It's dawn already. This is no time for sleeping." He glared at the two of them, then asked, "Where's Pigsy?"

Something crashed right near the edge of the clearing and Pigsy stepped into sight. He had gnawed his way through the entire trunk of a tree.

"Breakfast is the most important meal of the day," Pigsy said, then burped.

The Friar glanced at Nick. "Is that funny?"

Nick nodded and the Friar put on his best forced smile.

Nick patted him on the back as they headed toward Monkey. "You're doing fine. Just take it slow."

The Friar nodded like a puppy following a bouncing ball.

Thirteen

It took them most of the day to travel through the forest, and Nick was amazed at the stories Monkey, Pigsy, and Friar told as they walked. It was as if he were reading different versions of stories just like *Journey to the West*.

"We're almost to the Western Sea," Monkey said as they neared the top of a small hill. "The weather is warmer in this part of the world."

"Which means the women wear fewer clothes." Pigsy winked at Nick.

Actually, the only woman Nick wanted to see was Kwan. But so far there hadn't been a reason to call her.

As they crested the hill, Nick could see the walls and high watchtowers of a city perched along the shore of a dark ocean.

"The city of Jinping," Monkey said, pointing ahead of them.

But it became clear as they got closer that something was very wrong with this city. Ancient structures had collapsed roofs and patched walls, garbage lined the streets, and the people were old or disabled.

"What happened here?" Nick asked as they slowly walked into the city.

"I dunno," Pigsy said. "The women here used to be a lot better looking, that's for sure."

Monkey stopped and pointed ahead to a statue in the main square of the city. Nick knew at once it was the image of the fat Shu, the same man Kwan had shown him in their travels to the past.

"Shu and the Masters must have taken over the city," Monkey turned to Pigsy and Friar. "Come, brothers, let us give them hope."

Monkey strode toward the statue, with Pigsy and Friar right behind. Nick stayed off to one side and out of the way. As Monkey got near the big statue of Shu, he leaped into the air and kicked it, smashing it to the ground.

All the citizens stopped what they were doing, alarmed at what the stranger had done.

"Citizens of Jinping," Monkey shouted as the three of them struck poses where the statue had been, "I am Sun Wukong, the Great Sage Equaling Heaven. Take heart. We have come to end your days of suffering."

The crowd just stared.

One priest laughed. "Not the most attractive group of gods."

Pigsy shook his head. "Why does everyone always point that out?"

Monkey signaled the other two. As one, they sprang upward, doing two somersaults in formation while their weapons flashed around them. When they landed, the impressed crowds around Nick broke into applause. Even Nick was impressed. Clearly it was something the three of them had practiced a few times just for occasions like this one.

As the applause died down, the citizens started spewing hundreds of pent-up grievances at their new heroes.

"The demons have taken all our able-bodied citizens."

"Our children are sent to far-off lands to plunder sacred relics for the masters' treasure vault."

"If the children don't come back with something valuable, their entire family is executed."

Nick was stunned at the complaints and stories of abuse. He listened for a few moments, waiting for Monkey to speak, but clearly Monkey was overwhelmed by it all as well. Well, Monkey had said they were there to give these people hope. Nick figured he might as well start.

He moved over and jumped to the base of the statue beside Monkey, Pigsy, and Friar. "Citizens of Jinping," he shouted, getting their attention. "My name is Scholar From Above."

He could see the doubt in their faces, so he quickly added, "I know I don't look like a Scholar, but that's because I am just learning what it means to feel compassion. So trust me when I say we will rid your village of these demons or die trying!"

Around them the citizens of the city cheered and smiled and clapped each other on the back.

"Let's go," Nick said, and jumped down.

The other three followed him as the crowds parted for them to head toward the sea, where the demons lived.

"Good speech," Monkey said as they cleared the outer edge of the mob of people.

"I remembered this coach I had back in high school."

"Whatever." Monkey patted Nick on the back. "Now let's go see if we can live up to what you promised."

"So where do we start?" Pigsy asked as they headed for the edge of the water.

The ocean looked dark and dangerous. A dock and a paved roadway ran along the beach. Monkey led them out onto the dock over the water. It smelled of rot and dead fish, and Nick hoped it would hold them all.

"One of the citizens mentioned that the Masters have a treasure vault," Monkey said. "I'll bet that's where we'll find the manuscript. I'll go down first and study the terrain. Wait here for my signal."

Nick wasn't at all sure he liked the idea of Monkey going alone, but neither of the others objected, so he didn't either.

The crowds had stopped a hundred steps back up the road toward the edge of the city and were watching as Monkey dived in. They all made mumbling sounds.

Nick paced to the right across the dock while Pigsy, eating a fruit, paced to the left. Then they came back at each other, turned, and paced away. The entire time Friar stood like a stone statue, his face showing no emotion.

It only took four times back and forth before Monkey's cudgel exploded out of the water.

"Let's go," Pigsy said. "That's the signal."

"I just hope I can still breathe underwater," Nick said as he dived in and followed the other two to the bottom. Luckily, he could. Whatever Monkey had done to him seemed permanent.

Monkey stood near the entrance to a stone tunnel. Two octopus guards were tied up with their own legs and not at all happy about it. Monkey pointed inside and held his cudgel in ready position.

Nick, Pigsy, and Friar all drew their weapons and followed Monkey through the invisible shield that held the water out of the tunnel. They had just entered the Masters' lair. Nick really wished Kwan was with them now.

The entrance tunnel expanded into a massive Jade Tunnel, bending off and down to the right. Monkey led the way, with the Friar bringing up the rear. The Jade Tunnel looked as if it was the main corridor for the entire compound.

Almost instantly two bull-headed guards spotted them. Before either could call out an alarm, Monkey cut the face off the first one and then grabbed the horns of the second, smashing him into the stone wall so hard Nick doubted there was a bone left unbroken in the guard's body.

As they moved slowly down the Jade Corridor, Nick kept expecting something to jump out at them. But nothing did. Laughter sounded from down the hall, and the banging of dishes and pans came from off to their left. But no more guards. Weird.

After a hundred steps, the corridor ended in a large room. Against one wall was the statue of a giant turtle. Friar, without even questioning, moved up to the statue and pushed it aside.

Behind the statue, Nick could see a very narrow corridor, pitch black except for dozens of tiny lights.

"What are those?" Pigsy asked, staring into the darkness. "Jewels?"

Suddenly the lights moved at them, and Nick knew exactly what they were. Dozens of demon guards.

"I was starting to think they didn't care," Monkey said.

Nick thought he had stepped into hell. The guards seemed to come in four or five different ugly forms. There were bull-headed men with horns, wolf-guards like Nick had seen on Monkey's island, and a nasty-looking tiger-headed guard that moved with the speed of a cat.

Pigsy, his rake a blur, head-bashed demons as fast as they came at him, leaving them punctured and bleeding from dozens of holes in their skulls.

Friar Sand fought in a completely different way. He was more like an unstoppable machine, fighting in close, letting cudgels break off his skull and blades bounce off his skin as he cut down every monster that came in reach with his iron fists.

Nick managed to hold his own as well, letting the brush-pen do the work for him, just as he had done the night in front of Kwan. It was as if the pen had a mind of its own, seeing when a demon was coming in behind him and blocking the ax blow. Nick and his brush even managed to smash a few demon heads.

Monkey looked more like a martial arts movie in fast motion. He kicked, spun, chopped, and hit continuously, moving around the room, making short work of every demon he could find.

Finally, as Friar Sand knocked three demon heads together and let the bodies crumple to the ground, the big room was silent. Nick could feel his heart trying to pound right out of his chest as he looked around at the carnage the four of them had caused.

"A good fight is a thing of beauty," Pigsy said.

At that moment, Nick could only agree. It *was* a thing of beauty, and a real adrenaline rush at the same time.

Monkey motioned that they should follow him into the tunnel where the demons had come from. Still breathing hard, Nick stepped into third position behind Pigsy, and the four of them went the last fifty steps into the Master's secret treasure vault.

What greeted them there took Nick's breath away even more than the fight. There was more beauty and treasure than he could have imagined in one place. Some of what filled the massive chamber he recognized.

Prayer wheels from Tibet.

Hermaphroditic Hindu deities.

The tablets of the *I Ching*.

The bones of Taoist hermits.

The hundred-foot-long sleeping Buddha from Treasure Mountain.

Sand painted mandalas.

The mask of the Dalai Lama.

"Oh, my God," Nick said softly.

"Not just one god, Scholar," Monkey said. "All the gods of creation."

Nick could not disagree.

"By building this collection," Monkey said, "Shu and the Masters enhanced their own strength, harnessing the power of these relics for evil."

"Look." Pigsy moved to his right among the mass of treasures. "Over here!"

Nick and Monkey and Friar joined Pigsy as he stood in front of a golden pedestal on which lay a large, ancient book.

"Journey to the West," Pigsy said, reading the print on the cover, "by Wu Cheng-En."

"It's really here," Nick said, not believing that they had actually found what they had set out to find.

Monkey turned to Nick. "Take it, Master. It is your discovery, for your world."

Nick tried to keep his hands from shaking as he slowly reached out and took hold of the wonderful book. As he lifted it, something changed.

"The pedestal!" Friar said.

Nick grasped the book against his chest and stepped back, watching as the pedestal became a clear window into a dungeon cell below. There, against the wall, an emaciated old man hung, more dead than alive, as far as Nick could tell.

"Author Wu?" Pigsy asked, clearly stunned.

Now it was Nick's turned to be stunned. It was Wu. Wu had died in the beating Shu's men had given him that he and Kwan had watched, and then he had come here, to an afterlife where he was imprisoned by the same man who had killed him.

"He has been here all this time," Friar said. "The Masters must have captured him as well as his book."

"Is he still alive?" Nick stared at the bones and skin of the body hanging from the stone wall in chains.

"I bet there were times when he wished he was dead," Monkey said.

Friar smashed the pedestal to bits with one blow from his fist, and Monkey leaped into the hole, working quickly to release the chains that held the old man.

Nick kept the book against his chest, holding it with both hands, his brush-pen under his arm as he watched the scene in the cell below.

As Monkey worked, the old man opened his eyes. "Monkey?" he said, his voice a horse whisper. "Can it really be you? Or has my mind finally taken leave of its senses?"

"No, Great Author," Monkey said, "your suffering has come to an end at last."

Wu's eyes filled with tears. Joyfully, he took Monkey's face in his bruised and torn hands. "They captured me. No writer could imagine the torments I have endured over these centuries."

"It's our fault," Monkey said, "for ever losing sight of you. I swear I will pay back your suffering a thousandfold. But first we must get you out of here."

As Monkey lifted Wu out of the dungeon, Nick stepped back and looked at the book in his hands. Then, reverently, he opened one page, just for a quick peek.

The page was blank.

And so was the next page and the next page.

"Monkey!" Nick called out as Wu stood, his hand on Pigsy's shoulders.

Nick kept flipping through the book. Every page was empty. How could this be? He showed the empty pages to everyone.

"What's going on here?" Pigsy asked.

Wu let out a weak chuckle. "You're looking for my manuscript?"

With Pigsy's help, he hobbled across the large chamber a short distance. "You'll learn I still have a few tricks up my sleeve. That book in your hands is a decoy I made."

Wu climbed up a short ladder beside a ten-foot-tall urn, with Pigsy spotting him to make sure the old author didn't fall.

"The true manuscript I hid in here." Wu pointed at the urn. "And those criminals never figured it out."

He fought to remove the heavy cast-iron lid on the big urn, but couldn't.

"Monkey, will you help me?"

Monkey leaped to the top of the ladder.

Nick glanced at the decoy in his hand. None of this was making any sense at all. "You mean, Author Wu, that the Masters aren't on the verge of destroying your book?"

Friar looked at Nick, also clearly puzzled. How could the Masters be changing the world above if they were not threatening the real *Journey to the West*?

Nick knew something was very wrong. His little voice inside was screaming.

"All will become clear"—Wu smiled.

Monkey pulled the lid off the big urn.

"No!" Nick shouted.

"—right about now." Wu finished his sentence.

Two arms resembling clouds, one white, one black, shot out of the top of the urn, grabbed Monkey, and yanked him down inside, pulling the lid closed after them.

"Brother Monkey!" Friar shouted, and started toward the urn.

But it was too late. As the arms took Monkey into the urn, compartments opened everywhere around them, each packed with demons.

Hundreds of demons.

Nick, Pigsy, and Friar backed into a circle, weapons at ready, but it was far, far too late. They were outnumbered fifty to one. Any fight would be suicide without Monkey with them.

"I'm afraid we have been deceived," Friar said.

"You're working with them?" Pigsy asked Wu, who was still on the ladder beside the urn that had captured Monkey. "Why?"

"Don't be shy, my old friend," a voice said from behind the wall of demons.

Nick recognized the voice as the fat man Shu stepped forward.

"Modesty in the defense of tradition is no virtue," Shu said.

Nick's pen was taken from him, and a thick rope was wound around each of them, so tight that Nick almost could not breathe.

"Heavenly rope," Friar muttered.

Nick knew whatever *heavenly rope* was, it wasn't good.

Wu smiled, his broken teeth ugly and rotted. "It was the least I could do, Master," Wu said to Shu, "to atone for my crimes."

The jar holding Monkey started to shake as Monkey tried to escape. But no matter how much the jar rocked or jerked from Monkey's movements, nothing happened.

Shu laughed and patted the side of the urn. "One of my favorite treasures, and most useful as well. It is the jar containing matter and nothingness from Lion Camel Mountain."

Pigsy turned to Nick. "That's the only container that's ever been able to hold Monkey."

Shu turned to Wu. "And you got him in it," Shu said. "Who knows? In time, we may even honor you with the title Junior Master."

Wu bowed and then bowed again. "Thank you, great author."

"What do you mean?" Pigsy asked, clearly disgusted. *"You* are the great author."

Wu shook his head. "No, I have long ago come to accept the truth that during my lifetime, I failed to write anything of lasting value, because of my incorrect thinking and failure to follow the artistic principles set down by our Great Patriots."

Shu smiled after hearing Wu parrot his party line. It made Nick sick to see such a man of principles so beaten.

"It seems," Friar said, "that they have succeeded in brainwashing him."

"Wu." Nick tried to look into the eyes of the old man. "Your book *Journey to the West* is the one people still remember. Hardly anyone in the real world knows who the Masters were."

Shu suddenly looked very angry. One of the demons stepped forward and slammed the butt of a halberd into Nick's stomach. He doubled over, his air gone, pain filling every inch of his being.

Through the haze of pain, Nick heard Author Wu say, "No, no, that's not true. It can't be."

Nick managed to get a little air into his lungs, and the pain faded slightly.

Wu crossed to face Shu. "Master," Wu said, "I have stopped these thieves, as you ordered me to do. Now you will release them, according to your promise."

Shu laughed and again patted the urn holding Monkey. "Since when do promises made to criminals count? We have finally imprisoned the Great Sage Monkey. We're certainly going to try to take his *chi*."

Shu laughed, the sound echoing through the treasure of the gods. "It may take three, maybe four thousand years, but because of the Dragons

I have put in there with him, at least Monkey will be suffering that entire time."

As Nick watched, the urn shrank, and expanded, then shrank again, clearly showing the battle Monkey was fighting inside. They had to do something.

"But we had an agreement," Wu said.

"So what are you going to do about it?" Shu laughed at the old man. "Sue me in the court of the Jade Emperor?"

Shu's joke got all the demons laughing and barking and snorting, filling the chamber with the most horrific noise Nick could have imagined.

Wu turned and dashed for the ladder, climbing up to try to take the lid off the urn. "Monkey," Wu said, almost sobbing, "you must believe me. I meant you no harm."

The guards easily took the old man prisoner. Then Shu walked up to the Great Author and slapped him.

Wu bent his head, clearly defeated and ashamed.

Shu signaled his soldiers to take Pigsy and Friar. "Imprison them," Shu said. "And this time find a bigger mountain."

Then Shu turned and faced Nick. "As for you, human, you fought with surprising ability."

"Does that mean you're going to let me go?" Nick asked, knowing he wasn't going to get the answer he wanted.

"No," Shu said, "that means we can enhance our own powers by eating you."

Nick looked at Pigsy, then at Friar. "For the record," he said, "that's not funny."

A few dozen guards took the struggling Pigsy and Friar away as Nick tried to get free.

Shu stepped up to Nick and showed him a mirror. "Don't feel bad, human," Shu said. "The way things are going in your world, if you had returned you never would have recognized it anyway."

In the mirror was the image of Big Ben in London. The hands of the mighty clock were moving backward, and a mob ran wild in the streets.

As Shu turned away, Nick bowed his head. "Goddess, I need your help."

Shu laughed and turned back to Nick. "Don't bother trying to contact any of your influential friends. We constructed this bunker to block all communications with the outside world—except our own, of course."

Shu walked away, giving the guards their orders. "Tell the cooks to skin him alive and then fry him in refined butter oil. I want to crunch his bones."

"Goddess?" Nick whispered as they yanked him away from the urn holding Monkey. "Any time now."

There was no answer.

Fourteen

Monkey hadn't been so angry in his recent memory. And making him angry wasn't a good thing. This was the second time Shu had managed to trick him into a trap. It was going to be the last.

Four fire-breathing dragons constantly pounded at him from all sides of the urn, burning his fur in the tight confines simply because he had no place to dodge them. He had taken a moment to slay one when they first appeared, cutting off its head with his cudgel, but another had sprung up in its place. Clearly Shu's plan was to wear him down over a few thousand years until his *chi* was gone.

"Well, that's not going to happen." Monkey sliced off the head of another dragon that burned his back.

"Think!" he said aloud. He stopped and forced himself to look around. He knew the matter-nothingness urn he was in couldn't be broken out of. Every time he pushed upward, it just expanded. When he pushed the other direction, it shrank. The only way out was the top seal, and from what he could hear through the urn's sides, Pigsy, Friar, and the Scholar had been captured. Shu was going to imprison Pigsy and Friar under another mountain and eat the Scholar.

Not good. Not good at all.

He had to help them escape so they could pull the cork off the stupid urn and help him in return.

Outside he could hear the guards leading away his companions. He was going to have to act now, or soon it would be too late for them.

With all his strength, he launched himself at the cork of the bottle. It didn't open, but the urn expanded, smashing into the roof of the cavern. Rocks rained down on the guards, who shouted for him to stop.

"Ah, I may have found a way to help," he said.

Again, using all his strength, he smashed the nothingness urn into the ceiling of the treasure cavern.

And again.

And again.

Then he heard what he wanted to hear: the sound of water.

"Stop it!" the guards outside yelled.

"Oh, sure. Just let me out and I will."

One guard climbed on top of the urn to try to hold it down.

"Dumb, dumb, dumb." Monkey smashed upward again with all his force, expanding the jar until it slammed into the roof of the cavern, flattening the guard into a bloody pulp.

The cracks in the ceiling of the treasure cavern got wider and wider every time he hit it, until finally they opened, letting in the ocean from above.

Monkey smiled and shoved down on the floor of the urn, shrinking it down as small as he could. The water picked the urn up and floated it with the rest of the relics.

With luck, he had created enough of a diversion that his brothers would get away. And then they would release him so he could show Master Shu exactly what he felt.

The guards led Nick into a massive kitchen area that smelled of wonderful rolls and fresh meat baking in the ovens. Dragon-looking chefs filled the area, all working on different types of food preparation. The guards told one of the dragon-men in a tall white chief's hat what Master Shu had ordered.

"Wonderful," he said, looking at Nick. "Refined butter oil on this creature sounds delicious. Master Shu, as always, has wonderful tastes."

The guards pushed Nick toward a giant wok boiling with oil over a fire. Beside the wok was a chopping block. They picked him up and flopped him on it, face up, then held him in position. Nick had never been so afraid before. It felt as if his heart was going to explode from his body. He kicked and struggled with the guards, trying to get away, but their grips and the heavenly rope held him tight.

"Don't move," the dragon-chef said, sharpening a large knife on a wet stone beside Nick. "It only makes the meat tougher." To the guards, the chef said, "Now untie him. I don't want to have to pluck rope fiber from the skin."

The guards did as they were told, keeping him firmly in place.

Suddenly the entire kitchen shook.

The guards looked around, but the chef didn't seem to notice. He was more intent on the job at hand. Actually, so was Nick.

Again the kitchen shook, the rumble hard under the chopping block against his back.

And then again and again.

"I'm trying to work here," the dragon-chef said. "How can I make fine cuts of meat when the room is shaking?"

Nick hoped the shaking went on for a very, very long time.

Suddenly there was a roaring sound, as if a train was coming at them from the main tunnel.

Nick, the guards, and the chef all turned as one to see a wall of onrushing water, soldiers, and other debris ripping through the kitchen at them.

The wave hit, knocking Nick away from the guards and head over heals. But since he was still protected by Monkey's spell, he could breathe just fine under the water. Pigsy and Friar tumbled by, still tied up and at the mercy of the currents.

Nick grabbed a table leg and let most of the current pass him, then retrieved the chef's big knife from the floor and stood. The water was only waist deep and it didn't take him any time at all to find where Pigsy and Friar had been shoved into the dishwashing area of the kitchen. With a single slice, he cut both their ropes, setting them free.

Pigsy immediately dived into the water and came up with his rake, which had been shoved along with them. Nick looked around for his brush and found it floating nearby as well, along with the Friar's staff. They were armed and ready.

They took up fighting positions to face the rapidly recovering guards.

"A narrow escape," Pigsy said, sounding very happy. "Just like old times."

Master Shu sputtered to the surface near the door to the kitchen, stood, and looked around. "Stop them!" he shouted.

Still dazed and waterlogged, a few guards tried to do as Master Shu ordered, but the three of them cut the demon guards down easily. Nick stood with his back to Pigsy and Friar so they formed a three-sided defense and fighting machine.

Finally, more and more demons arrived, wading through the water and surrounding them by sheer numbers.

Shu moved toward a corner where a few other Masters had gathered in the slowly deepening water. One of the Masters had a firm grip on author Wu.

"We now have no other choice," Shu said to the other Masters. Over the water-filled room, his voice carried and Nick could hear every word. "We'll head for the throne room and call upon the Jade Emperor for help."

The other Masters nodded at the plan as Shu pushed open a panel embedded in the rock. Clearly the tunnel beyond the panel had been dry; Shu and the Masters were immediately sucked in by the rush of water moving to fill the space.

The water pulling on the guards knocked many of them off their feet, giving Nick, Pigsy, and Friar the upper hand in the fight for the first time in minutes.

"This way." Nick pointed back to the main corridor outside the kitchen.

In the hallway, the water was so deep the three of them had to swim, fighting the current to get back to the treasure vault. Dozens of demon soldiers were right behind them, but clearly no better swimmers than Nick and Pigsy and Friar.

Finally they reached the treasure vault. The water was pouring in from a dozen cracks in the ceiling right over where the urn had been.

"Brother Monkey's still trapped inside that jar," Pigsy said, half-walking, half-swimming toward where the urn had been. But it wasn't there.

The water must have knocked it away," Nick said. He dived under, searching through the debris for any sign of the urn. Nothing. Just ruined treasures, now lost forever.

When he surfaced, Friar and Pigsy were looking just a little worried. At least a hundred demon soldiers had made it into the room and had formed a circle around them.

"Put your hands behind your heads," one of the demons ordered.

"Oh, sure, so I can be cooked and eaten," Nick said. "I think I'd rather die trying to kill you."

"So would I," Pigsy said.

"I will fight with you, Scholar," Friar said.

Nick caught sight of a tiny urn floating a foot away. It was Monkey's jar, shrunk down to less than an inch in size.

Nick grabbed the jar just as the soldiers started to move closer to attack.

He quickly pulled off the lid and tossed it away. For a moment he thought he might have gotten the wrong urn. Then a jet of smoke fired out of the tiny jar and turned into Monkey, his cudgel moving like a helicopter blade, his eyes burning red.

"Think he's angry?" Pigsy asked, smiling at Nick.

At the sight of Monkey walking across the top of the water at them, the entire contingent of demon soldiers screamed and turned to flee. But they were standing in deep water, and Monkey's blade was acting like a propeller, churning up and spitting out everything in its path.

Pigsy, Nick, and Friar sauntered behind Monkey, letting him do all the work. As far as Nick was concerned, Monkey deserved the fun and needed to get some of the anger from being tricked out of his system. And killing demon guards who had taken him to be eaten was the perfect way, as far as Nick was concerned.

Pigsy laughed. "When word of our victory gets out, we are gonna meet so many girls."

The image of Kwan flashed back into Nick's mind. There was only one girl he wanted to meet again, preferably with lots of time and in a very private place.

Monkey finished his slicing and dicing of the hundred remaining demon guards, then turned to the three of them. "Any idea where Shu and the Masters went?"

"I saw them get swept down a tunnel off the kitchen," Nick said.

Without another word, Monkey turned and led them down the main corridor and into the kitchen, where the dragon-chefs were trying to save some of the pots and pans from the rising water. They retreated as the four entered.

Nick pointed to the open panel in the stone wall, and Monkey dived in, followed closely by Nick.

It didn't take them long to reach a private room, very antiseptic in feel even completely underwater. There was no one there, only the remains of a pedestal where something had been ripped off the floor.

"There." Monkey pointed at a glowing area of rock in the floor.

"Protected by magic," Pigsy said.

Monkey ignored him and smashed at it with his cudgel, doing no damage at all.

Friar motioned for Monkey to move aside, then took his staff and smashed down into the stone just beside the red glow. The rock shattered as he kept pounding, digging down past the magic seal, until there was a hole big enough for them to swim through.

Again Monkey took the lead, with Nick close behind.

The room that greeted them this time looked like what Nick figured a survivalist hideout might look when flooded. There were cases of food and a massive stockpile of weapons. But what was really odd was that Shu and the Seven Masters, along with Author Wu, were huddled in one corner, inside a large bubble of air that was keeping the water out, clearly by magic.

Monkey, Nick, Pigsy, and Friar all moved through the bubble and stood in front of them.

"There it is," Pigsy said, pointing at the pedestal one Master was holding.

Nick couldn't believe what he was seeing. This was clearly the real manuscript for *Journey to the West*, imprisoned under a glass dome. But the manuscript looked terrible, a sticky mess with leeches crawling all over it.

"By the gods," Pigsy said, "it's almost gone."

"Author Wu," Nick said, staring at the old man standing to one side of Shu, "how can you just stand there beside the people who would do something like this to your book?"

Wu glanced up at Master Shu, then looked at the floor.

"Shu," Monkey said, "give us the book now, as well as Author Wu. We will treat you more kindly than you have treated them."

Shu smiled at Monkey. Nick didn't much like

that smile at all. It wasn't the kind of look a man who was trapped would give to his captors.

Shu glanced around at the other Masters, then back at Monkey. "What do you think, boys? Should we do it?"

The Masters clearly pretended to give serious consideration to the question. Then, as one, they said, "Nah."

Monkey looked at them, his eyes red with anger. "I was hoping you would say that."

His cudgel became a blur of motion around him as he stepped toward the Masters.

Suddenly a voice filled the air. "Cease and desist."

A half-man, half-lion materialized between Monkey and the Masters, wielding what looked to Nick to be some sort of document.

Monkey stopped in mid stride.

Shu rushed forward, half angry at the new arrival. "Took you long enough to get here. Damned bureaucrats."

Shu snatched the document from the new arrival and looked it over.

"Who the hell is he?" Nick asked.

"The Imperial Crier," Friar said. "A messenger from the Jade Emperor, who rules over all gods and immortals."

Shu nodded and mumbled something that Nick thought sounded like "Perfect." Then Shu fixed his seal to the paper.

"The pleading's been generated in quadruplicate," the Crier said. "Please make certain you affirm each copy."

Shu shook his head in disgust and did as he was told.

The Crier gathered the copies and put them all together.

"Are you done now?" Monkey asked, his cudgel spinning as if it were anxious to cut into the Masters.

"Yes, quite." The Crier shoved a copy of the paper in front of Monkey's face.

"What am I supposed to do with this?" Monkey asked.

Clearing his throat, the Crier read from another copy. "By order of the Jade Emperor, whose holy word gives all subjects cause to fear and tremble, all hostilities must immediately cease, pending settlement of this pleading in the Court of Heaven."

Nick could not believe what was happening.

Friar took the paper from the stunned Monkey and looked it over, then turned to them. "It seems the Masters are suing us in the court of the Jade Emperor. They want to stop the Scholar from taking the manuscript back to his world above."

"You're kidding," Nick said.

Friar looked at Nick, his face serious. "I have not yet learned to kid."

Fifteen

Frustrated, Nick paced back and forth in the large conference room just down the hall from the Court of Heaven in one of the Six Western Palaces, as Monkey had called them. The room was big, with leather chairs and a massive table. There were even snacks for Pigsy.

They had been taken there by the Crier after the reading and had been told that in a short time they would be informed as to when the trial would take place and where. Now they were just waiting.

Kwan had joined them on their arrival, but had said little, and Nick was so angry he hadn't felt like talking to her.

"This is just great." He paced along one wall behind where Kwan and Friar sat at the table. "We're seconds away from victory and all of a sudden we're outfoxed by some *legal maneuverings!*"

He actually shouted the last two words.

"Nick, please," Kwan said.

"Your world is no better than mine." Nick kicked a chair and sent it spinning.

"I'm afraid immortality is no guarantee of good character." Kwan didn't look up at him.

"The Masters can't possibly win this case. Right?"

No one answered him.

"I mean, my world is about to slip back into the Dark Ages. Doesn't anyone here care?"

Again, without looking up, Kwan answered his question. "Except for Bodhisattvas, no spirit may travel to the world above without permission from the Jade Emperor. Most beings haven't seen your world in a thousand years. They don't understand the harm such an action would cause."

"But why would any immortal want to see *Journey to the West* destroyed?"

"It's a book about Monkey." Kwan glanced over to where Monkey sat silently. "The fact is, Monkey's never been the most popular deity among the other gods."

"They think I'm arrogant," Monkey said, shaking his head. "Can you imagine that?"

Nick stared at Monkey, then at Kwan, who finally had looked up at him. "So this decision is going to turn on his popularity?" He turned and dropped down into one of the empty chairs. "We're screwed."

"The Jade Emperor will pronounce judgment," Kwan said. "He is a fair ruler, but he believes Author Wu should have the final say over the fate of the manuscript."

Friar looked at Nick, then at Kwan. "We're screwed."

Nick could not believe any of this. "Deep inside, Wu can't really want to see his book destroyed. If only I could get to him somehow. Just a few minutes alone. I know I could snap him out of it."

Nick looked around at each of his companions. "Come on," he said. "You people are gods. Can't you figure out a way?"

Monkey, Friar, and Pigsy all turned as one to look at Kwan.

"Goddess," Monkey said, "could you disguise the Scholar with a spell?"

Kwan looked at Monkey, clearly shocked at the idea. "That would be using my powers for deception. I would be breaking all the holy rules."

"Rules, schmules," Pigsy said.

"He is the Scholar From Above," Friar said.

"Don't you care about him at all?" Pigsy asked.

Kwan looked over at Nick. He could see her eyes starting to tear up. Clearly she cared for him and wanted to help.

"I can't," she said softly, looking away. "I must keep my vows."

With that she got up and fled from the room.

Nick glanced at Monkey, then at Friar, then knew he had to go after her.

He jumped to his feet and ran out. Many different types of creatures filled the massive hall, and he could see Kwan ahead, moving off into a side corridor.

All the doors along the side corridor were closed and looked unused. He caught her easily near the end, where the corridor stopped at an emergency exit.

"Goddess?"

She kept staring at the exit door, not really moving. But he could tell she was fighting something big inside.

"What's going on?" he asked. "It's like you are afraid to even look at me."

He put his hand softly on her shoulder and turned her around. She looked up at him, and he knew she had been crying.

"Talk to me," he whispered. "Don't shut me out."

She took a deep breath and nodded. "Nick, this thing between us. It can't go on. You must understand."

"I understand that what I feel is impossible." He smiled at her, then went on. "But all the most beautiful things are. Someone told me that once. Someone I love."

He leaned forward to kiss her, and for an instant he could feel her giving in to him, moving toward him. Then, as if something yanked her back, she moved away.

"No. It's over. It has to be."

She turned and started back down the empty side corridor toward the crowded main hallway.

He knew how she really felt. She was being forced to act this way, and he would wait, find a way around what was stopping her from showing him her true feelings.

"What about saving the manuscript?" Nick asked. "Is that over, too?"

She stopped, but did not turn around to face him, as if doing so would weaken her resolve.

"Nick, I can't get you in to see Author Wu. That would be a violation of heavenly justice."

Nick laughed, the sound carrying down the narrow corridor. "So we're going to hang the fate of my world on the testimony of someone who's been brainwashed? You call that justice?"

She turned around and faced him, staring into his eyes intently. "What makes you so certain you could change Author Wu's mind?"

Nick shrugged. "I'd tell him how much his book means to people in my world. How much it meant to me."

Kwan looked into his eyes, her gaze softening.

"It was the first Chinese book I ever read," Nick said. "In comic form, when I was in high school. Up until that point, I was like most kids. China didn't mean anything more to me than Charlie Chan or Fu Manchu."

He let himself remember, the feelings as real as if they had just happened. "When I began to read about this Monkey who broke all the rules, pissed people off, but who did it with a higher purpose and a sense of humor, it made me feel as if I could do something with my life as well."

Kwan stared into his eyes as the memory faded. He could see that she understood, that she really did care. And behind all that, she really did love him.

He stepped forward and took her hands in his. "I'm trying to do something now. Will you help me?"

She sighed.

It was the most wonderful sigh he had ever heard.

They had waited until early evening, when they hoped Shu and the other Masters would be out partying, to try to approach Wu. Monkey had managed to climb down on top of the guest house that the Masters were staying in while waiting for the trial to start. Now Monkey, Kwan, Pigsy, and Friar all huddled with Nick behind a large chimney.

"You ready?" Monkey asked Nick. "I don't think they're going out."

Nick nodded and turned to Kwan. He wasn't exactly excited about going in with all the Masters there, but if he had to, he would.

"If anyone finds out I used my powers for deception . . ." Kwan's voice trailed off.

"I won't tell anyone," Monkey said. He turned to Pigsy. "Will you?"

"Never," Pigsy said.

"I will not," Friar said.

Kwan shook her head and then put her palms together. Nick watched as she began to chant. A moment later a beam of light came from between her eyes and covered him.

The next instant he was looking at his friends from a completely different perspective, and he was flying fast and quick.

He was actually a fly!

"This is really wild!" he shouted, testing his limits.

"Slow down!" Monkey whispered. "It's harder than you think to—"

Nick missed a quick corner he was trying to make around Kwan's shoulder and smashed into the pavilion chimney.

"—steer."

"Be careful," Kwan whispered as Nick shook off the shock of the impact and headed toward the open window below.

"And whatever you do," Monkey said, "stay off the dog doo-doo."

"Yeah, right." Nick doubted any of them heard him, since he was so small and too far away.

As he neared the window, the front door of the pavilion opened. Nick landed on the top of the open window so he could watch and listen.

"We'll be back after dinner," Shu said, standing half in, half out of the room.

"Yes, Master," Wu said. "I'll have tea for everyone, Master."

Nick felt disgusted at the Great Author acting as a servant to such slime.

"Why do I have to stay?" one of the other Masters asked.

Nick recognized him from a picture as the one they called Master Skeleton. He fit the description, since there wasn't much skin over his bones, and no fat at all under his skin.

"Can't we just lock him in?" Skeleton asked.

"Master," Wu said, "I promise I will not show my wretched face outside."

"That's right," Shu said. "You won't. In our

bunker all thinking is correct. Up here, the air itself is filled with sinful temptations.''

At that the Masters left, leaving Skeleton and Wu alone.

Nick watched as Skeleton plopped himself down on a Tang dynasty day bed in front of a round mirror that had been brought from their bunker. "Keep your mouth shut and don't move," Skeleton said to Wu.

Wu sat down in the window seat right below Nick and took a deep breath of the fresh evening air. "Don't worry, Master. I'll be happy just sitting here."

In the mirror, the image turned to what looked like the Mongolian desert, where a line of telephone poles stretched into the distance. Skeleton laughed as if watching a sitcom, as, one by one, the poles disappeared. The guy was actually getting enjoyment out of watching Nick's world vanish.

Nick let go of the windowsill and flew down to a point near the Great Author's ear.

"Author Wu, I must speak with you," Nick shouted, as loud as he thought he dared.

Wu didn't move, so Nick buzzed past his ear again. "Author Wu. It is I, the Scholar From Above."

Wu's hand flashed out faster than anything Nick had seen and grabbed him.

Nick thrashed around for a moment, then stopped trying to fly. The massive hands of the old author looked like they were going to flatten him dead. "Wait!" he shouted as loud as he could. "I'm not an ordinary fly."

Wu, who clearly hadn't heard Nick's shouts, whispered into his hands, his breath like a hurricane of rotting teeth. "Don't worry, little fellow. I know what it's like to fear for your life."

Wu thrust his palm out the window and released Nick.

Nick couldn't believe he was suddenly free. He tumbled for a moment before realizing he had to fly.

Nick swung around, got his bearings and went back to the old author. "Author Wu!" Nick shouted as loud as he could while making a tight circle in the air near the author's head. "You must listen to me!"

Wu turned and stared at the fly, clearly not believing what he had heard.

Nick pushed on. "I'm a human from above! Our entire world will suffer if your book is destroyed!"

Wu glanced over at Master Skeleton, then whispered, "Then my book is known?"

"It's one of the most beloved books in the world!" Nick shouted. "The Masters have brainwashed you with lies. Please don't let them destroy it!"

Wu put his face in his hands. "I just don't know what to believe any more."

"Wu!" Nick shouted. "Look at me. Look at me!"

Wu looked up into the tiny human face on the fly.

"I devoted my entire life to the study of your book! You were given the greatest gift known to man, the gift of creation. Don't throw it away!"

"How can this be?" Wu asked.

"Who are you talking to?" Skeleton stood and moved toward Wu.

"No one, Master," Wu said as Nick darted away. "Just myself."

"Didn't I tell you to keep your mouth shut?" Skeleton asked, clearly angry he had been disturbed. "And close the window. You're letting in flies."

Skeleton grabbed a flyswatter and moved to hit Nick.

Nick, moving as fast as his little fly wings would take him, tried to circle back and head out the window, but he missed, banging hard into the window ledge.

Skeleton swung and barely missed, knocking over a large vase with a loud crash.

"I'll get you!" Skeleton shouted, now enjoying chasing a fly more than watching the world above being destroyed.

Nick managed to avoid two more wild swings from the Master, but then a hand reached up and grabbed him. Author Wu's hand.

"Please, Master," Wu said. "Allow me."

Nick could see through the cracks between Wu's fingers that Wu was headed for the window.

"Wait a second," Skeleton said.

"Damn," Nick muttered. "So close."

"I like to pull their wings off," Skeleton said.

Nick looked at his wings, attached where his

arms used to be. He didn't like the sound of that at all.

Author Wu's hands were opened slightly and Nick sprang upward, trying to make a break for it. But Skeleton was too fast. He got a hold of one wing, then the other, spreading Nick out and bringing him up close to the ugly, thin face of the Master.

"Hey," Skeleton said, "you're that human. The one who came with Monkey!"

Nick wanted to take a bow and then kick the guy in his bony face, but his wings were pinned open in a very painful way.

He was doomed. There was no doubt about it.

"Let him go!" Kwan's voice said from behind Skeleton.

Kwan materialized on her cloud right in a place where Nick could see her. She was the best thing he had seen in a long time. She placed her palms together and a ray of light hit Nick.

Suddenly he was no longer a tiny fly, but full size, and Skeleton had his arms pinned.

"You heard me," Kwan said. "Release him."

"Who's gonna make me?"

Monkey, followed closely by Pigsy and Friar, burst through the door.

Skeleton shoved Nick toward his friends and stepped back. "You know what this is, don't you? Witness tampering. Once word gets out about this, Goddess, you ain't gonna have a prayer in the world."

Nick looked at Kwan, her face firm in the presence of Skeleton, but clearly not happy.

"Let's go before I cut this bony Master up myself," Monkey said, "and feed him to the dogs below."

Kwan turned and went out the door, with Nick right behind her. All knew they had lost the gamble.

There was nothing any of them could say.

The next morning they were all summoned to the big hall and Confucius's offices. But only Kwan and her assistant were asked inside. The four of them were forced to sit and wait and listen to the shouting from Confucius. And there was a *lot* of shouting, all one-sided.

"The entire Order of Bodhisattvas has been disgraced by your actions!" Confucius shouted at one point.

Nick wanted to go in and defend her, take the blame, but Monkey held him in his seat. It had been explained to him a few dozen times last night that going to her aid would only make matters worse. It was the way of the gods, and she was the most powerful of them all, so she took the blame.

Kwan never said a word that they could hear.

Finally the door opened and Kwan came out, followed by Whitesnake, her assistant.

Whitesnake glanced at Nick with a look that said clearly, *This is all your fault.*

Nick knew it was his fault, in a way. He had

been the one who thought he could change Wu's mind about destroying the book.

Kwan and Whitesnake walked past them and outside, so they all followed.

On the front steps in the bright morning sunshine, Nick stopped Kwan, turning her so that she faced him. "I'm sorry. I didn't understand the risks you would be taking."

Whitesnake stepped between them, pulling Kwan away.

"The Bodhisattva must return immediately to the convent," Whitesnake said. "She will see you at the trial tomorrow. She is lucky to even be allowed to be there."

As Whitesnake led her away by the arm, suddenly Kwan twisted free and looked back at Nick. "I'm glad I did it, Nick. I would do it again."

Nick looked into her eyes and he knew now what was there. Love and belief. And if she could maintain that after risking what she risked, then so could he.

Whitesnake formed a cloud under both her and Kwan and sped them into the sky.

Nick watched until they vanished.

"She has given a great deal for this cause," Pigsy said.

Nick nodded. "She has."

"And we must not give up this fight," Monkey said. "We must prove we are worthy of her belief."

"I agree," Friar said.

Nick glanced at Monkey, surprised. "Do you have an idea?"

Monkey shook his head. "Not a one. But I'm sure something will come to me."

"It always does," Pigsy said. "It always does."

But for some reason, this time Nick had the feeling that nothing would.

Sixteen

Nick, in his wildest imagination, never could have dreamed up what now lay before him. Double roofs of a pagoda so large they could have covered most of Manhattan Island floated in the sky, supported by columns of clouds. Long lines of deities of every shape, size, and religion wound through the gardens around the massive hall, hoping to gain admission.

Inside, the Hall of Miraculous Mist was even more impressive than outside. The walls seemed to fade into a white mist on all sides, and into clouds above. Heavenly Soldiers were mounted on gray clouds, and a Dragon Throne was perched high on a brightly colored cloud dais that looked like a combined sunset and sunrise.

When Nick, Monkey, Kwan, Pigsy, and Whitesnake entered, the galleries on multilevels of clouds were already packed with immortals and gods awaiting the start of the trial.

Nick led the way as they took their positions behind a smooth, carved-jade table. Whitesnake stood just behind and to the left of Kwan.

Nick couldn't help gazing around at the pageantry of the Jade Emperor's court. It felt as if the entire universe was watching this trial. For all he knew, it might be.

At least a dozen bull-headed drummers pounded away on Chinese kettledrums as the Imperial Honor Guard marched in. Nick knew the guard represented every major family of deities. The parade looked more like the opening ceremonies of the Olympics than the start of a trial, and it lasted a good fifteen minutes.

To Nick's left was another table just like the one they stood at. As Nick watched, Shu and the rest of the Seven Traditional Masters filed in from a hidden door, with Author Wu in the middle. Clearly Wu had been beaten after Nick's visit last night, but except for a black eye, there wasn't much obvious damage. Nick tried to catch Wu's attention, but the author kept his head down, his eyes focused on the table in front of him.

Finally all the noise and fanfare came to an abrupt halt as the Imperial Crier flew in from the blue sky above and landed at the cloud dais. The colors flashed around him, and every being went silent. Nick thought the entire place could hear his heartbeat in the stillness.

"Buddhas, Bodhisattvas, Gods, Immortals, and Citizens, all bow low before the Protector of Celestial Skies, Judge over the Living and the Dead, the Holy Light of Paradise, the Source of Divine Wisdom . . ."

The list seemed to go on and on, like the announcements at a prize fight.

Monkey yawned beside Nick, and Kwan jabbed him in the ribs.

Finally, the Crier got to the final part. "His Majesty, the Jade Emperor."

Trumpets from every side of the massive courtroom blared. Lightning in all colors slashed from the cloud roof over them. It was an amazing light show, and Nick was watching it when Monkey pulled him down to a bowing position.

Nick couldn't help it. He had to watch, so even bowing, he stared upward as best he could.

Carried in a sedan chair by at least twenty flying dragon-bearers, the Jade Emperor entered, trailed by at least fifty thinly dressed maidens. The guy looked almost human, maybe in his sixties, wearing a yellow robe and headdress that couldn't be light. He had a wispy mustache and really, really long earlobes.

The bearers put the sedan chair on the Dragon Throne as the trumpets hit the highest note possible and stopped.

Confucius moved out onto a lower bench area to the right of the Emperor and cleared his throat as everyone took their places.

Nick and the others had seated themselves when Confucius said to them, "Rise."

Nick and the rest did, as well as Shu and the Seven Masters. A tiger-clerk moved to present papers to the Emperor as Confucius started to read.

"Our business here today is the case of Shu Chung-Shing and the Seven Traditional Masters versus the Scholar From Above, concerning the fate of this manuscript titled *Journey to the West.*"

Confucius indicated where the manuscript

was being carried to the front platform by another tiger-clerk. Nick was stunned at the shape of the book. It was still covered in leaches and poisonous talismans, and now it was barely visible at all.

"Master Shu, you may give your remarks," Confucius said.

Shu thanked the Emperor and half the deities for their time, then moved out in front of his table, pacing. Nick listened as he outlined his and the other Masters' beliefs that the wonders of China should be maintained, hitting the nationalist cord so often used by tyrants.

Then Shu finally got to the point. "But why, Your Majesty, do we seek to destroy this obscene book?"

Shu moved in front of Monkey and jabbed a finger in Monkey's face, daring the god to bite it.

Nick put a hand on Monkey to make sure he didn't.

"Because this Monkey is an affront to traditional Chinese values. His story, told in that book, corrupts humans, encouraging them to thumb their noses at authority, to take foolish chances, to see themselves as—dare I say it—*individuals.*"

Nick was stunned at how Shu spit out that last word, as if it were the worst swear word in existence.

Monkey stuck out his tongue.

Shu bowed, thanked the Emperor for his time, and moved back to his table, where he was patted roundly on the back by the other Masters.

Confucius nodded for Nick's side to go ahead. They had decided, as was custom, that the highest ranking should speak for them. That was Kwan. Besides, Nick figured that if everyone below was in love with her, chances are a few in the heavenly court were as well.

Kwan stepped from behind the table, went through the ritual thank yous, then got right to the point. "Master Shu says *Journey to the West* should be destroyed because the Monkey Spirit encourages freedom and individuality."

She paused to look directly at the Emperor, and then at the crowd. "Are such qualities anti-Chinese?"

Again she paused. Nick could not believe what a wonderful speech she was making. She had the rapt attention of everyone in the massive space.

"Of course not," she almost shouted, setting everyone back at the sudden change in volume. "What did Lord Buddha himself say? *Only when each individual has the courage to follow his or her own path, only then will the world become enlightened.*"

Nick could see the Emperor nodding in agreement. That was good. Very good.

Kwan thanked everyone again, as was custom, and returned to her spot beside Nick. He so wanted to turn and hug her, kiss her for her wonderful speech, but he didn't. It was not the time or the place.

"I thank you both for your considered arguments," the Jade Emperor said, his voice full and rich and carrying to every corner of the space. "This case has aroused great passion on both sides. however, I hold to my previously stated position. Only Author Wu, the creator of the work, has the authority to decide where *Journey to the West* should reside—indeed, whether it should continue to exist at all. Today, we are happy to see him among us."

Wu smiled at the Emperor, stood, and bowed. But before he could say anything, Master Shu stood.

"Master Prime Minister!" Shu said, addressing Confucius instead of the Jade Emperor.

Kwan looked at Nick, then at Monkey with a worried expression.

Suddenly Monkey slapped his head, as if remembering something clearly.

"Please forgive our unconventional request," Shu went on, "but may we approach the throne? With fear and trembling?"

Confucius looked first at Shu, then at Kwan, then nodded. "You may."

"What's happening?" Nick asked as Shu moved up to the throne in front of Confucius.

Kwan shook her head. "I don't know."

"I do," Monkey whispered. "Confucius is working with the Seven Masters."

Nick stared at him as if he had gone nuts.

"That can't be," Kwan whispered back. "He would never risk his position with the Jade Emperor."

"Oh really?" Monkey said. "Then tell me who else has the power to send Heavenly Soldiers to help Shu take over my island. That's been bothering me since it happened."

Nick suddenly remembered that detail as well. Who could have done it to help Shu? He looked at Kwan. "When we were fighting in Shu's bunker, they were very confident that the Heavenly Crier would come to save them. Who has the power to send the Crier that quickly?"

"Very confident," Monkey whispered. "And only Confucius has that power. Now it all makes sense."

Kwan started to open her mouth, then understood what Monkey and Nick were saying.

And if they were right, there was nothing good in store for them now.

The conference between Shu and Confucius seemed to be over. Shu moved back to his table, then said, "Most High Emperor, Prime Minister, the Masters would like to call one witness."

"This is not going to be good," Monkey whispered.

"None of us are humans," Shu said, "so how can we know for certain how they themselves feel about this book? Therefore, the Masters would like to call to the stand the Scholar From Above."

Of all the things Nick had expected, that was not one of them. He sat there stunned. It was clear from the silence in the massive space that everyone else was stunned also.

"I don't like this," Kwan Ying whispered.

"Do I have a choice?" Nick asked.

"No," Kwan said.

Nick stepped around the end of the table and

moved to where Confucius indicated he should stand, on a large cloud-like pedestal that quickly formed a witness box around him. He could feel a thousand gods and immortals staring at him. In all his life, he had never felt so exposed and on the spot. He took a deep breath and tried to center himself, just as he had learned on that cliff edge.

"For the record," Shu said, moving up in front of Nick, "you are a human being?"

"Most people would say so."

"And what is your opinion of *Journey to the West*?"

Nick looked at Shu. The guy had to be the stupidest prosecutor in the entire world to open the questioning with that. Nick looked directly at Author Wu. "Quite simply, it changed my life. It gave me purpose, taught me how to live."

Wu gave Nick a tiny smile. Maybe there was hope.

"Then you don't believe this book should be destroyed?" Shu asked.

"Of course not. Author Wu's book is sacred to humans. It is more precious than gold."

"Then why, Scholar From Above," Shu said, stepping up closer to Nick, "did you destroy your only copy?"

Everyone in the massive spaced turned to their neighbors in surprise. The rumble was so loud, it sounded like thunder. Confucius banged a gavel and brought everything back to order.

Nick was stunned. He didn't know what to

say, so he said the first thing that came to mind. "That's not true." But he knew it was true.

"So you deny the charge?" Shu smiled.

"Yes. I mean, no," Nick said.

"Which is it, Scholar?" Shu asked. "The credibility of your entire case rests on your reply."

The weight of a thousand stares pressed down on him. He could hardly breathe. Author Wu was sitting bolt upright, listening intently.

Nick glanced at Kwan. The pain and sympathy were clear on her face. She also knew the answer. It was impossible to hide anything from the gods.

"OK, I did it," Nick said. "But it wasn't because—"

"Didn't you come to hate the book?" Shu shouted over the loud rumble of the audience reacting to Nick's confession. "Didn't you come to see it as evil? Something that had led your life astray?"

Nick knew the answer, but he didn't dare say it, not now. "You know, I don't honestly recall. I just know what it means to me now. And what it means to the world."

Shu produced a circular pocket mirror. Around the vast hall a hundred large mirrors came into existence, showing exactly what Nick was seeing, only larger, like a big screen at a football game.

"Well," Shu said, "let me refresh your memory."

In the mirror was the image of himself, back in college over ten years ago. The scene was back in his room, just after Linda had left. He was angry, and his friend Andrew had just come in and was trying to calm him down.

Nick watched in horror as the scene unfolded. The most important day of his entire life spread out on big mirrors for every god in creation to see.

Nick had already torn the Chinese print to shreds when Andrew came in.

"What are you doing?" Andrew asked.

"What does it look like?" Nick said. *"She left me for that damned professor."*

"But that's no reason to go trashing your entire life."

"No?" Nick shouted. *"Can you think of a better one?"*

"Screw her," Andrew said. *"You've got to show her you can rise above this."*

Nick picked up the bound report on his desk. It was a copy of his dissertation, In Search of the Monkey King. *"That's exactly what I intend to do."*

He tossed the dissertation in the trash.

"What are you doing?"

Nick waved away his friend. *"I don't need that anymore."*

"Whoa, whoa there," Andrew said. *"You're on the verge of becoming one of the world's great China scholars."*

"Like that's a way to make a living," Nick said, disgusted. He reached up on the shelf, took down the copy of Journey to the West, and held it up for Andrew to see. *"This is what got me into trouble in the first place. Through this I met Linda. I've wasted so much time."*

He took the book and ripped it down the spine.

Andrew tried to stop him, but Nick pushed him away.

"I wish I had never seen this thing. That it never even existed."

The image on all the mirrors froze on him throwing the book into the garbage.

The silence in the massive hall was so intense it felt like a wall.

Nick had never felt so ashamed of an action. How could he have let his emotions over someone like Linda destroy so much?

Finally, Shu said, "That will be all."

The mirrors disappeared.

Across the space, Author Wu sat with his head down, his last belief clearly shattered.

They had lost.

And the world above had lost everything as well.

Seventeen

Nick felt dead. That simple. Completely dead. On the witness stand Author Wu stood, his eyes focused down in front of him.

"Tell us what you feel about your work *Journey to the West*," Shu asked.

"The book is a bane to mankind," Wu said, his voice as dead as Nick felt. "Though I will always bear the shame of having written it, I will do whatever I can to atone for my crimes."

Beside Nick, Monkey sprang to his feet. "Emperor, he's been brainwashed by Shu and kept prisoner for the last five hundred years."

"One more disturbance," Confucius said, staring at Monkey, "and your entire team will be removed."

"Author Wu," the Jade Emperor said, "have you been held against your will?"

Nick perked up at that question.

"I have lived among the Masters, Your Highness," Wu said, clearly prepared for the question. "It has been my privilege."

"Are you willing to affix your seal to a statement affirming this?" Confucius asked Wu.

"Unfortunately, I do not have a seal," Wu said. "But I will sign my name."

Wu took out a brush-pen with his name carved into the wood as Confucius produced a document.

"Man, that was convenient," Monkey said. Then he shouted, "In the name of Buddha, tell them the truth, Author Wu."

Kwan Ying leaned over Nick and put her hand over Monkey's mouth. "They'll throw us out of the courtroom."

"Like we got a lot to lose," Monkey said.

Kwan sat back, clearly struck by what Monkey had said. All Nick could think about was that it was all his fault.

Beside him Kwan stood and spoke. "Author Wu, don't let them destroy your book. Billions of humans will suffer a terrible—"

Wu put his hand up and stopped Kwan. "Lord Confucius, I do not wish to hear more from that table."

Confucius banged his staff. "So you will not. Remove them from the courtroom."

A Heavenly Regiment of Varjipranis moved to escort them out. Varjipranis were monster, bare-chested fighting machines with fez-like caps. No one in his right mind would tangle with one of them.

As Nick stood, Confucius broke in. "No, let him stay. One defendant must remain to hear the Judgment of Heaven."

Nick sat back down as the others left. Now, alone at the massive jade table under the gaze of all the gods and immortals, he felt even smaller and more stupid. A moment ago he hadn't thought that was possible.

Outside on the front steps of the Hall of Miraculous Mist, Friar, Monkey, Pigsy, Kwan, and Whitesnake all stood.

"We were so close," Monkey said. "So close."

"How could the Masters have found out about the Scholar's past?" Friar asked.

"The same way we knew about it," Monkey said, disgusted.

"Goddess," Whitesnake said, "we have lost this battle. Now listen to me. You have got to get back to work and put this entire matter behind you. There has already been talk of demoting you to a mere immortal."

"I don't care."

"What?"

Even Monkey was surprised.

"Let them do their worst," Kwan said. "What does it mean to be a Bodhisattva, anyway? Spending eternity helping others, but the one time I feel something myself, they hem me in with regulations."

"Shhh." Whitesnake looked around. "You never know who might be listening."

"Nicholas Orton came here to help us," Kwan said. "Honestly, to help me. And look what they have done to him by dragging his past, his worst moments, out for everyone to see. If this is the way Heaven acts, I don't want to serve here any longer. I'd rather speak the truth, no matter what it costs me."

"Goddess, don't—"

"I can't help it, Sister," Kwan said. "I love him."

All the gods recoiled in shock. Monkey actually sat down on the steps, his head in his hands.

Whitesnake shook her head sadly. "You have spoken the words that must not be uttered."

"Ask me if I care," Kwan said.

"I fear you will care," Whitesnake replied. "I fear you will."

On the high Dragon Throne, the Jade Emperor was giving his judgment.

"And so, Heaven has no choice but to accede to the wishes of the work's author and creator."

Nick stared at Author Wu, sitting on the end with the Masters. He seemed like a completely broken man.

The Jade Emperor continued. "The human, Scholar From Above, will return immediately to his own world without the manuscript. *Journey to the West* will be returned to the possession of the Seven Traditional Masters, who may complete their efforts to destroy it."

"All hail the infinite wisdom of the Jade Emperor!" Confucius declared.

The trial was over. They had lost.

The world above had lost.

The trumpets blared, the lightning started, and the drums pounded. Dragon-bearers lifted the Emperor's sedan chair as maidens in thin veils fell into formation around it.

But all Nick could do was stare at the Author Wu. Suddenly he realized a large tear was rolling down the old man's cheek.

It was like a slap on Nick's face.

Instantly Nick knew what he had to do.

He sprang to his feet, elbowing the massive guard standing behind him so hard the guy fell over onto his back.

Nick grabbed the brush-pen out of his pocket. "Grow!"

With the largest leap he had ever made, he sprang toward Shu and the Author Wu, his brush-pen a full weapon in his hand.

He landed among the Masters, shoving them hard, catching them all by surprise. He grabbed Wu's arm. "Sorry, but this is a rescue, whether you like it or not."

As the recessional fanfare devolved into a chaotic mess above them, Confucius shouted, "Apprehend him!"

A hundred Heavenly Soldiers descended from different directions. One arm holding onto Wu, Nick got ready to defend himself, the brush forming a blur around him.

Then, as he thought that flight would be a better form of battle at the moment, his brush lifted them into the air.

Nick managed to keep his grasp on Author Wu's thin arm as the brush, spinning like a propeller blade, whisked him up and into one of the high galleries, far above all the soldiers.

But the soldiers could fly as well, and they were not far behind.

With his brush-pen moving faster than it had

ever moved before, he fought his way to the upper exit and parted the sea of immortals jamming together to get out of the way.

By the time most of the Heavenly Soldiers had reached the gallery, Nick was outside in the courtyard.

He dashed around the corner, carrying the old author like so much baggage. There on the steps were Kwan, Monkey, Friar, and Pigsy.

"A little help here," Nick shouted as two guards stepped in front of him. He took one out with the first spin of his brush and knocked the other into a tree with a second move.

"Nick!" Kwan shouted. "What are you doing?"

"I've got to show Author Wu the truth," Nick said. "Would you help me take him to my world?"

"Are you insane?" Whitesnake asked. "It would mean going to war against all the powers of Heaven."

From around the side of the massive courtroom, Heavenly Troops poured into sight— dragons, Varjipranis, and brightly costumed officers, all welding battle-axs, lances, halberds, and long-poled maces.

Monkey smiled as Friar and Pigsy leaped to Nick's side. "Us against all of creation. I like those odds."

"Join them," Whitesnake said to Kwan, "and you throw away everything you've worked for over a thousand incarnations."

"Dear Sister," Kwan said, "I'm already losing my powers. I might as well follow my heart."

Nick handed Wu to Kwan Ying.

"Don't I have any say in the matter?" Wu asked.

"No!" all four of them said at once.

The battle began.

Nick was starting to learn to trust his weapon, and himself. The four of them formed a perfect fighting machine against the Heavenly Warriors, with Kwan and Wu protected in the center. At one point Nick downed four assailants at once, two with his pen and two with kicks.

Kwan Ying defended herself and Wu as well as soldiers got through. Twice she tried to generate a cloud to get them above the fight, and twice it failed. Nick knew her powers were failing.

One Varjiprani got through Kwan's defense and caught Wu on the side of the head, knocking the old author out.

"Help Kwan," Nick shouted, and as a unit they dropped back toward her.

Again she tried to generate a cloud, and again she failed.

"Buddha, please help?" Nick heard her say.

A cloud appeared beneath her and Wu. Whitesnake smiled at Kwan.

"He's not exactly Gandhi, you know."

Kwan nodded.

"Good luck," Whitesnake said.

The cloud lifted Kwan and Wu up over the fight.

"Head for the Western Gate," Monkey shouted. He grabbed Nick's arm, barely ducking a blow from Nick, who hadn't seen what Monkey was doing. "You're getting better."

"Thanks," Nick said.

With a mighty leap, Monkey and Nick somersaulted over the pagoda rooftops toward the gate.

Nick glanced around as Pigsy and Friar did the same. Kwan and Wu, on the cloud, were close behind.

And right behind them were hundreds of Heavenly Soldiers.

From what Nick could tell, the soldiers were going to catch Kwan and Wu before they reached the gate.

"Help them," Nick shouted to Friar and Pigsy.

Both turned, saw the problem, and fell back, swatting Heavenly Soldiers out of the sky and into the homes below. For a short time, it must have seemed as if it were raining soldiers in heaven.

Ahead Nick could see the Western Gate, a magnificent structure supported by two jade columns. From the gate, guards flew up to meet them. They were dressed in fierce costumes, elaborate headdresses, and colorful banners.

Monkey turned to Nick. "These guys think they're wounded if they break a nail."

Nick laughed as Monkey pulled a fistful of hair from his chest and said, "Change."

Scores of tiny monkeys attacked the guards, pulling off headdresses, ripping banners, and just playing havoc with their costumes.

The guards fell back, clearly too busy fighting

the small battle of their appearance to fight the larger one.

"Those gates are indestructible," Monkey shouted as he veered upward. "We'll have to go over."

But as they went up, so did the top of the gate. Finally, Monkey stopped. "I hate Miraculous Growing Mortar."

Behind them Pigsy and the Friar were fighting a fallback battle against a growing force of Heavenly Warriors.

"The gates are indestructible?" Nick asked. "How about the walls?"

"They are, too," Monkey smiled at the idea. "But the jade columns supporting it all aren't."

Using one foot to hang on to Nick, Monkey smashed his cudgel into one of the columns supporting the Western Gate.

Whack after whack, each blow sent a quake through all of Heaven.

Cracks appeared in the column as Nick fought off one guard who got through.

Monkey kept on pounding.

"We hate to rush you!" Pigsy said, as he and Friar and Kwan backed up against the wall.

Monkey smashed his cudgel one more time into the column and this time it broke, cracking down the center and toppling away.

Slowly, the column fell, causing all fighting to stop for the moment as they watched a sight no one had ever seen. Part of the wall of heaven was coming down.

Then it got worse.

The second column on the other side of the

Western Gate, no longer able to support the weight of the monster gate alone, also crumbled and broke.

And then the arch that supported the walls on both sides of the gate could no longer stand alone.

Section by agonizing section, the walls of Heaven fell.

"Let's go!" Monkey shouted.

A moment later they were outside and at the edge of the gigantic cloud on which the Heavenly City rested, far above the world in the tomb.

Nick looked back at the cloud of dust and the destruction they had caused.

Monkey smiled at him. "I think our work here is done, don't you?"

"I'd say we've done enough," Nick said.

"More than enough." Kwan smiled at Nick.

"Is that funny?" Friar asked.

Nick laughed. "In a way, yes."

As one, with the still unconscious Author Wu in Kwan's hands, they dived off the edge of the cloud and headed for the world below.

And from there, it was only a short stair climb back to the real world. Nick just hoped they weren't too late.

Eighteen

"I want to see what has happened," the Jade Emperor ordered. With Confucius close behind, the porters rushed the Emperor in his sedan chair to a place where he could see all the walls of heaven—or what was left of them. Now only the four gates remained standing.

The Emperor shook his head in anger and disgust. "In the future," he said, "it might be wise to construct gates which are not so indestructible. Take me back."

Inside the Hall of Miraculous Mist, the Emperor looked around. The fighting in here had taken its toll as well. Around the Emperor were the Masters, Confucius, his Secretary, and an array of Heavenly Soldiers.

"Prime Minister Confucius," the Emperor said, "you will assemble one hundred thousand heavenly troops to apprehend the rebel spirits."

"With all due respect, Your Highness," Confucius said, "I believe we can resolve this matter much more simply."

"How?" the Emperor asked.

"All I require is a handful of your finest warriors—the Two Heavenly Kings and the god Er-lang."

The Heavenly Kings were Lute and Umbrella, massive humans with costumes and faces on which characters of Chinese Opera were modeled. The god Erlang was brightly dressed, with a third eye in his forehead.

"Erlang," Confucius said, "is the only god among us who has defeated Monkey before."

"Only these to capture Monkey's entire band?" the Jade Emperor asked, disbelieving.

"Yes, Your Highness. If this fails, then we can bring on the thousands of troops. But first let us try the simple method."

The Jade Emperor nodded. "But I want results. It's going to take a hundred years to repair all this damage."

"Results you will get," Confucius said. "On that I can promise."

In a clearing on the side of the mountain where Nick first entered the Emperor's tomb, Author Wu slowly came around. Kwan held him in her lap, patting the bump on his head with a damp cloth. Monkey had created the same golden steps to the World Above Gate that he had offered Nick what seemed like an eternity ago. Now Monkey, Pigsy, and Friar stood guard, waiting for them all to go.

As Wu opened his eyes and sat up, Nick knelt in front of him. "Author Wu, please hear me out. Come back to my world—"

Wu shook his head and pointed a finger at

Nick. "I won't believe another word from your lips. Do you deny that you cursed my book?"

"No," Nick said, the pain of the memory and what had happened in the courtroom stabbing through him. "But I was wrong."

"He spoke the truth," Kwan said, "about the importance of your book to humans above. If you'll just let us show you."

"You want me to testify against the Masters," Wu said. "You're trying to brainwash me."

Wu pushed Kwan away and stood. "Just let me find a ray of sunlight where I may sit until they come to arrest all of you traitors."

He started to move away, then stumbled and fell.

Nick moved to help him while Kwan put her palms together and started to chant.

Nothing happened.

She tried again, but still nothing.

She stared at her useless palms. Then slowly tears formed in her eyes.

"Monkey, can you help him?" Kwan turned and ran into the trees.

"Goddess?" Nick followed her, knowing she needed him.

It took him a hundred steps to catch her. She had stopped to lean against a tree. He came up behind her as she was wiping tears from her eyes.

"I know the trouble you've gotten yourself into," Nick said. "And I'm sorry. I didn't mean to do this to you."

She turned, trying to smile at him. But he could tell it was only for show.

"Don't say another word," she said, touching his lips with her fingers. "I don't want to hear about any of that."

She put her arms around his neck and pulled him close. "I feel I can face any punishment," she said, "so long as I'm looking into your eyes. Kiss me again. Please?"

He pressed against her, his mouth matching hers, his lips basking in the wonderful feel of her lips. He didn't care about anything but holding her.

Finally, she broke the kiss and looked at him. "Know this much, Nicholas Orton. No matter what happens, I love you."

She released him and turned and moved away.

Nick felt himself in so much shock, he couldn't even move to follow her. He just watched her walk away through the trees.

"Hold it right there," Monkey said behind him.

Nick turned and stared at Monkey. Then he broke into a smile that felt as if it would break his face wide open. "She said she still loves me."

"Well, she's wrong."

"What?" Nick stared at Monkey.

Monkey clapped his hands together, as if trying to get Nick to wake up. "By the gods, what a mess. You don't get it, do you?"

"Get what?" Nick demanded. "She said she loved me. And I love her. What is there to get?"

Monkey shook his head as if talking to a

child. "When a Bodhisattva falls in love, she loses her powers."

Suddenly Nick realized what really was going on, and why she had run off crying. She wasn't being punished by the Emperor or her convent. She was giving up everything she knew because of her love for him. That thought rocked him clear to his center and took his breath away.

"Haven't you noticed her loss of power already starting to happen?" Monkey asked. "She can't even fly anymore."

Nick nodded. He had noticed. He just hadn't known the exact reason, with so many things happening to them.

"So you're going to make sure she doesn't destroy herself completely," Monkey said. "Understand?"

Nick looked at Monkey. "No, I don't understand. How can I change—"

"Break her heart."

Nick looked at him as if he were speaking Greek. Kwan was the woman he loved more than anything else in the world. How could he break her heart?

"Come on," Monkey said, "you humans are good at that sort of thing, aren't you? Tell her you don't love her. End this now."

"Are you crazy?" Nick asked, slowly getting angry. "I love her. There is no way—"

"Millions of humans turn to her for comfort," Monkey said. "Do you know what would happen if their prayers suddenly went unanswered?"

"Shouldn't that be her decision?"

"Arghhh." Monkey was obviously not happy with the way the conversation was going. "Don't you care about your own world? Or her? You think instead of being a goddess, she's going to be happier being your *girlfriend?*"

That question stung, but Nick wasn't about to let Monkey get the best of him. "If she really loved me, then maybe. There's only one way to find out. I have to talk to her."

Monkey stepped into Nick's path. "Now is not the time to talk. Now is the time to do. While she still has some hope of regaining her powers."

"Get out of my way," Nick said. "This is between her and me."

"You're going to throw her over one day anyway," Monkey said. "Why not do it now?"

"What makes you so sure?" Nick demanded, his anger taking over.

"That's the way it is with you humans," Monkey said, disgusted. "You fall in love, then out again. The story of your lives. Well, I'm not going to let you add the Goddess of Mercy to your list of victims."

"Yeah," Nick said, "as if a Monkey could understand any of this."

Nick tried to push past Monkey, but Monkey raised his cudgel. "I'm your teacher. For once in your life, obey me."

Nick shook his head. "There comes a time when a student stops listening to his teacher."

"I'm still waiting for you to *start!*"

That was too much for Nick. His pen grew in his hands and he charged Monkey.

Monkey didn't move and Nick hit him squarely on the head, cleaving Monkey's head into two halves.

Nick instantly was horrified at what he had done. "Monkey?"

"How little respect you have for your teacher," Monkey said out of one side of his cut-in-half head.

He turned and stormed off.

"Wait!" Nick shouted.

"Do what you want," Monkey said without turning back or fixing his own head. "Your world can go back to the Stone Age for all I care. Never again will I share my wisdom with such an ungrateful child."

"Come back!" Nick said. "I'm sorry."

But Monkey was gone.

Nick turned and headed in the direction Kwan had gone. One thing at a time. First he had to talk to Kwan. Then he would repair the rift with Monkey.

It took a few minutes, but he finally caught up with her. She didn't see him approach and kept trying to conjure a cloud, her palms pressed together, her eyes closed, her chants becoming more and more insistent.

Nick stopped and stepped behind a tree, watching.

Over and over again she tried, each time producing a few pitiful whiffs of clouds that were quickly scattered to the breeze. Finally, she bowed her head and cried, her sobs echoing through the trees.

Monkey had been right. Her love for him was

causing her nothing but pain. And Nick could never allow that to happen. He loved her too much.

He turned and moved away before she saw him, her sobs echoing in his mind.

Nineteen

Friar Sand and Author Wu sat in the sunlight, staring out over the beautiful valley that lay beyond. For the past few minutes they had been talking about their captivity.

"For me," Friar said, "it was the sunrises I missed the most." He remembered the sunrise just after Monkey and the Scholar had released him from five hundred years under the mountain. It had been glorious.

"Sunrises are beautiful, yes," Wu said. "But the stars. I missed the stars and the night sky."

"I know what you mean." Friar plucked a flower from the grass and offered it to Wu. "Have you had the chance yet to simply smell a flower?"

Wu shook his head and took the blossom, marveling at the beauty of it. Then he inhaled, long and slowly. "This is the smell of freedom."

"Yes, it is," Friar said.

"On days when I had cleaning duty, the Masters would say, *Time to tend the flowerbeds*. Then they would toss me into the latrines. That was a source of great humor for them."

"I do not find that funny," Friar said, staring

at the Great Author. Maybe he had missed something again.

Wu looked at the Friar, then nodded. "You're right. It wasn't funny."

For some reason, that comment made Friar feel as if he had done something important. He didn't know what. It just felt important.

Nick managed to find his way back to the clearing where Pigsy was grazing on berries and Friar and Author Wu were sitting in the sun. From the scene, Nick never would have thought that they were about to be attacked by Heavenly Soldiers. Nick just hoped Monkey wasn't so angry that he wouldn't help when the fighting really got going or that he hadn't gone too far away to know when it did.

Right now Nick had to focus on trying to save his world. Saving the Goddess from herself would have to come later.

"OK, Wu," Nick said, kneeling beside the great author. "Everything I touch turns to mud. I admit that. I've made more mistakes in my life than you could count. So forget about me. I'm not the issue here. Don't make humanity suffer for my crimes. Please come with me up those stairs."

Wu stared at Nick for a moment, then glanced at Friar.

"You should go," Friar said.

Wu nodded and turned back to Nick. "OK, let's go."

Nick, about ready to keep arguing, took a moment to comprehend what the Great Author had said.

Wu pushed himself to his feet and started toward the World Above Gate staircase.

Suddenly an icy wind whipped out of the sky, pushing the author back.

"What's going on?" Nick shouted over the sudden gale as Friar climbed to his feet and Pigsy came running.

Pitch-black clouds were boiling in the sky, sweeping in their direction like an angry thunderstorm, turning the wonderful sunlight to darkness.

"They have come," Friar said.

Kwan darted from the woods, running toward them as fast as she could. Nick moved to help Author Wu remain on his feet and headed toward the staircase. The wind was so strong, it was almost like walking against a wall.

"Goddess," Friar shouted to her. "Author Wu is ready to go with the Scholar."

Kwan nodded. "We can still make it to the World Above Gate before the Emperor's forces arrive. I'll fly us up."

She started to put her palms together, then remembered.

"Friar, can you take us to the gate? Monkey can keep the soldiers busy."

"Monkey's gone," Nick said. "There's not time to explain. Let's go."

With a wave of his hand, Friar created a cloud under Kwan, Wu, and Nick. Then, with Pigsy and Friar as rear guards, they headed up the stairs toward the portal.

Suddenly in the sky two figures appeared out of the dark clouds. One was the Lute King and one was the Umbrella King, both closing fast.

"Oh, no," Kwan said, seeing who they were running from.

Nick knew of them as well, and knew their reputations. Things were not looking good.

Suddenly, a smile on his painted face, the Lute King began to strum his Horrible Magic Lute.

Wu, Nick, and Kwan covered their ears, doing everything they could to avoid the awful music, yet keep the cloud moving forward up the staircase.

"It's the worst thing I've ever heard!" Pigsy shouted behind them.

Above them the Lute King played blissfully, a virtuoso of sound only in his own mind. To the rest of the world, it was enough to stop rain in the sky and freeze even the most beautiful sunlight.

"I think I'm going to pass out!" Wu said.

"I think I'm going to throw up," Pigsy said.

A black cloud suddenly took on another form to the left of them, behind Friar's back.

"The warrior Erlang," Kwan shouted.

"Friar!" Nick shouted. "Behind you!"

Too late. Erlang tossed a mighty thunderbolt that smashed into the back of Friar's head, knocking him end over end through the skies. Nick watched in horror as Friar eventually fell unconscious on the rocks below.

Erlang tossed another thunderbolt that struck the cloud they were on. It was knocked out from under them as if it had never been there. The three of them tumbled to the staircase below.

As Nick hit and rolled, he saw Monkey coming in to help. Erlang saw him at the same time, and the two mortal enemies turned to face each other. Faster than the eye could follow, the two flew at each other, their eyes ablaze with hate.

The head-on collision flashed white and the shock wave crumbled mountains. Nick couldn't see what happened to either of them.

On the rocks below, Friar stirred and jumped to his feet, back in the battle. But suddenly he was pulled away from the staircase.

Behind him the Umbrella King had opened his giant umbrella. Holding onto the pin at the top, the Umbrella King wielded it like a giant vacuum cleaner, sucking up anything at which the umbrella was pointed.

Before Friar had a chance to react, he disappeared into the blackness of the umbrella.

Nick scrambled up the staircase to Wu, who looked unhurt. "Can you climb?"

The old man nodded. "Anything to get away from the music."

"Then go," Nick said. "We'll be right behind you."

Wu nodded and started up.

Nick jumped down the twenty steps to where Kwan sat, her hands over her ears, rocking back and forth.

"Come on!" he shouted, pulling her up to her feet.

"I can't stand this." Her face was white, and

she looked as if she would pass out at any moment. For some reason, maybe because he had listened to so much bad rock and roll, the music wasn't getting to him as much as to her.

The Umbrella King turned to aim his giant suction umbrella at them on the stairs. From down the mountain, Pigsy flew upward and grabbed on to the handle of the umbrella with his teeth.

No matter how much the suction, Pigsy refused to let go, keeping the umbrella pointed away from the staircase, at least for the moment.

"Come on!" Nick shouted over the music and wind.

"Go without me!" Kwan shouted back, keeping her hands over her ears.

Nick shook his head. "You've given strength to billions of souls," Nick shouted. "Now, Goddess, heal thyself!"

He swept her up in his arms and ran up the stairs toward Wu. Behind them the music pounded at him, beat at him.

He glanced over his shoulder as Pigsy kept fighting, eating at the umbrella handle as if it were a tough snack, not letting go.

In the skies, Nick could see the battle between Monkey and Erlang, their weapons clashing in lightning-like strikes that filled the heavens.

Wu reached the landing to the World Above Gate Pagoda just a few steps before Nick and Kwan. The cloud Friar had made for them was there at the top of the stairs, so Nick laid Kwan on it, turning his back on Author Wu for an instant.

One instant too long.

Confucius and Shu suddenly appeared right behind them. Shu pulled out a sword, smiling at what he was about to do.

As Nick turned around, Shu ran his sword through Wu's back.

"Oh, my God!" Nick shouted.

"No!" Monkey's shout echoed over all the land.

The great author's golden *chi* was running out of his wounds, sparkling as it hit the air.

Shu pulled the blade from the Great Author's back and the old man staggered forward and dropped into Kwan's arms on the cloud, clearly dying.

Nick stared at the author, then turned to Confucius and Shu, his brush-pen full-sized in his hand. "I don't care if you're immortals, I swear I'll kill you."

"Cease your useless posturing," Confucius said. "You need me to heal him before he loses his *chi*."

Nick stopped, clearly stunned.

Confucius turned to Kwan, who was holding the dying man. "Unless, Goddess, you think you can do it."

She looked at Wu, then at Nick. "Put down your weapon, Nick."

"No!" Wu said, his voice firm. "I want to know the truth. Show me the world above."

"We can't," Kwan said, tears in her eyes. "We can't lose you."

"Even if I die," Wu said, "my *chi* lives on forever. Goddess, you know my heart."

She looked at Wu. Then, after a long moment, she nodded. "Nick, use your weapon."

"Gladly," Nick said, his pen moving faster and faster as he started toward Shu and Confucius.

Shu took up a defensive stance while Confucius held up his hand. "Wait, you can't attack me. I'm an officer of the Jade Emperor."

"So?" Nick's pen smashed Confucius on the side of the head, sending him flying off the staircase and onto the rocks below.

With two more quick moves, he sent Shu into the air as well.

"Done," Nick said, leaping onto the cloud with Kwan and Wu.

"I do not have much time," Wu said. "And I do not wish to die listening to such awful music."

In the distance below, Pigsy was weakening, slowly being sucked into the blackness of the umbrella. Monkey, who had tried to come to help Nick and Kwan and Wu, had been struck down by Erlang and was being tied up with Heavenly Cord.

"Now," Nick said.

Kwan nodded. With what power she had left, she directed the cloud through the portal and into the World Above Gate.

Twenty

The cloud Nick, Wu, and Kwan were on went through the gate and appeared in the air in front of the Terracotta Warriors, passed over a stunned guard, and flew out the main door in the darkness of the night. Kwan turned the cloud to head for the city of Xian, then went back to treating Wu's wound.

Nick sat beside them and watched as the golden *chi* ran from Wu like a steady stream. "Can't we do anything to stop the bleeding?" If bleeding was what Wu was really doing. Wu had already died hundreds of years before, so Nick wasn't exactly sure what was happening now.

Kwan ripped a strip of cloth from her robe and tried to hold it against the wound, but the *chi* flowed through it, as if it weren't there. "I don't know what to do," she said, panicked. "I've never worked like this before."

Wu patted her arm. "I've made my decision," he said. "Just help me get comfortable."

Kwan shifted so Wu had his head on her lap.

He nodded his thanks, then pointed upward. "Stars haven't changed much, I see."

Nick glanced up, then at the rapidly approaching lights of the city and the light of the coming dawn on the horizon. "What can we do?"

Wu smiled at him. "Keep your promise and show me your world."

Nick looked up at Kwan, then nodded. "That we will do."

Kwan took the cloud in over the city and they moved Author Wu to the edge so he could see down. They supported him between them so he didn't have to strain.

Below them the main streets were filled with cars, scooters, and bicycles as the early morning traffic thickened. They sped over major streets and still-sleeping neighborhoods. In one area, workers were unloading crops from a railroad boxcar.

"There is so much food," Wu said.

"Enough to feed almost all of China," Kwan said. "It is a time of plenty."

As their cloud moved over an area near the airport, a giant plane roared in for a landing. Nick pointed to it. "Over five hundred souls in that plane. Nowadays, gods and goddesses aren't the only ones who can fly."

Suddenly, just as the plane was about to land, it flickered and vanished.

"What happened?" Wu asked.

Nick stared at where the plane had been, then turned to Wu. "That's what we've been trying to tell you."

"All these wonders of the modern age will disappear," Kwan said, "if your book dies."

"My book?" Wu whispered, looking at the cars and tall buildings and lights. "How can it be *that* important?"

"We will show you," Kwan said.

For the next two hours, as the sun came up and the day began for all of China, Nick, Kwan, and Wu toured the countryside. At one spot they found a school where the children were playing before going inside. A number of them were pretending to be Monkey, Friar, and Pigsy, all wearing cardboard masks.

"For centuries," Kwan said, "the children of China have learned the stories that you wrote."

Wu said nothing, but Nick could see a tear in his eye.

Kwan steered the cloud near a university, where through one window they saw a professor lecturing with a large banner in front of the room showing Monkey.

"They study them as adults as well," Nick said. He didn't mention that he had done that until that fateful day when he had made his stupid mistake and quit over Linda.

Kwan guided the cloud over the countryside, then back to the city. As they passed over a neighborhood, Nick caught sight of something and indicated Kwan should go closer. It was a boy reading a comic book. Not just any comic book, but the comic version of *Journey to the West.*

"Your book has inspired not only the rulers of China," Kwan said, "but the ordinary people who have looked to Monkey for generations. Your book inspired them to dream of things new and better and to believe that those dreams could come true."

Kwan took the cloud back up high and let it drift over the land.

"This is a world beyond my imagination," Wu said. "And yet it is clear I am a part of it."

"Very much so," Nick said.

"But all this will die unless we act," Kwan said. "Do you understand now?"

Wu nodded. "What a fool I was to believe the lies of the Masters. I let them take from me my faith in my own vision. If only I could undo my mistakes."

Nick glanced at Wu, who was looking very pale, then to Kwan. "Can we get Author Wu back to change his testimony before his *chi* is lost?"

"No," Wu said, "I do not believe that is possible."

He pointed down to where his legs were becoming transparent.

"Dear Buddha," Kwan said. "If only I had my powers."

Nick didn't know what to say.

"Do not fear, children," Wu said. "Everything will be all right."

Nick could not imagine how at this point.

"Of course it will, Author Wu," Kwan said.

"I only wish I could find some way to thank you." Wu looked first at Nick, then at Kwan. "You have risked so much because of my foolishness."

"Showing you the truth has been our greatest reward," Kwan said.

Nick had to agree with that.

"Scholar," Wu said, "reach into my robes. Quickly, before they are gone as well."

Nick did as he was told.

"Reach in the pocket. You will find an item of great value."

Nick closed his fingers around what felt like a brush-pen and pulled it from the Author's pocket.

"That is the pen with which I wrote *Journey to the West,*" Wu said. "Keep it as your inheritance."

Nick was stunned. He could see the characters of Wu's name carved into the wood. "I couldn't."

"Someone once told me something very important." Wu pushed away Nick's attempt to give the pen back. "The gift of creation is the greatest blessing known to humans. Such a precious thing must never be thrown away."

"I told you that," Nick said.

Wu smiled. "I knew it was someone very wise."

As Wu spoke, his entire body was becoming transparent.

"That pen is an even trade," Wu said, "for the gift you gave me. The knowledge that my life had meaning."

Slowly the Great Author's body faded away.

"I am free." His voice sounded joyous as it echoed around them and over the countryside below. "Now I am finally free."

Then he was gone.

"No!" Kwan said, sobbing.

Nick just sat there on the cloud and stared at where the Great Author had been a moment before, the pen in his hand a hard reminder that it had all really happened.

Author Wu was gone.

"If I still had my powers," Kwan said, between sobs, "not only would Wu still be alive, but he'd be able to testify for us, to save the book and your world."

She smashed her fists over and over into the cloud, as though hitting something very hard.

Nick tried to comfort her, but she wasn't listening.

"And now look at me! What good am I to anyone? I can no longer even help myself!"

Nick said nothing. There was nothing he could say. He held her, letting her sob into his shoulder.

Finally, she took a deep breath and straightened up. "I must go back now to accept my punishment."

"You have to?"

"Yes," she said, simply and firmly, leaving no doubt. Then she tried to smile through the still-flowing tears. "Please stay here, where you'll be safe. None of this is your fault."

Nick laughed, the sound harsh and bitter. "It's all my fault and we both know it," he said. "Come on, we'll face the music together."

Twenty-one

The minute Nick and Kwan appeared back in front of the destroyed walls of the Heavenly City, they were bound with heavenly rope and escorted by at least fifty Varjipranis guards into the Hall of Miraculous Mist. There they were placed behind the jade table that was starting to become familiar. The Emperor was on his Dragon Throne, looking just plain pissed.

Confucius sat in his position. A bandage around his head, a brace on his neck, and crutches beside his chair gave a clear indication of his injuries from his little fall. Even Shu, at the other jade table, looked beaten and bruised. It made Nick happy to see that he could inflict the damage he had. Those two deserved so much more.

Confucius rose and balanced himself on his crutches. "Your Highness, we have succeeded in apprehending the last of the rebels, at great cost."

"What cost?" Nick asked loud enough for almost everyone to hear, including the thousands that were again cramming the galleries. "We surrendered."

Kwan went to shush him, then shrugged. It didn't much matter at this point.

"Bring in the others," Confucius said.

An entire regiment of Varjipranis entered, bringing in Friar, Pigsy, and Monkey. They were also bound in heavenly rope, and Monkey did not look happy at all.

After the three were led to a position beside Nick and Kwan, Confucius got right down to the business at hand. "Violators of the Heavenly Will, do you have anything to say for yourselves before the Jade Emperor pronounces judgment?"

Nick glanced at Monkey, then at Kwan. Neither seemed to be about to speak up.

"Very well," Confucius said.

"Wait!" Nick stepped forward around the end of the table and dropped to his knees. "Emperor, I was the one who kidnapped Author Wu. These warriors were only trying to help me. I beg of you, let them go. If anyone deserves to be punished, it is me."

"And," Confucius said, "you will be."

"And one more thing." Nick got to his feet.

"Now what?" Confucius asked, clearly annoyed.

"Someone else here deserves to be tried." Nick glanced over his shoulder at the table where the Seven Masters were sitting. "Master Shu took Author Wu's *chi* in cold blood."

"That is a lie!" Shu shouted, jumping to his feet. "First they violate Heaven's Will, then they hurl false accusations at the righteous."

"The human speaks the truth, Your Highness," Kwan said. "I saw the entire thing."

"As did I," Monkey said.

He managed to bang his staff. "Silence! Silence!"

He looked directly into Nick's eyes. "I was there also, Your Highness, and will tell you the truth. Author Wu was wounded accidentally, in the heat of battle. I could have saved his *chi*, but instead these criminals pulled him away and forced him into the World Above Gate. When I moved to save Author Wu, this one knocked me off the Gate."

Confucius pointed at Nick.

The crowd made rumbling noises.

"The matter is resolved," Confucius said, banging his staff.

The Emperor shook his head in sadness. "The death of Author Wu is a terrible tragedy. In the absence of more conclusive testimony, I must accept the word of my Prime Minister."

Nick started to say something, then just shut his mouth. In all his wildest nightmares, he never could have come up with something so stacked against them.

"It is a crime of the most serious order to disrupt this court," the Emperor said, going on with his speech.

In Nick's shirt pocket, something moved. The only thing in that pocket was Wu's brush-pen. It was moving on its own accord, and since Nick's hands were tied, he could do nothing about it.

"Therefore," the Emperor said, "we have no

choice but to impose the harshest available sentence upon the rebels."

The brush-pen sprang from Nick's pocket and flew into the air, circling around and around like a nimble bug.

"What is that?" Monkey asked.

Nick only smiled.

"Shoot it down," Confucius ordered.

"Wait!" the Emperor shouted.

"Is that what I think it is?" Kwan asked, looking at Nick. All Nick could do was smile and nod.

The pen had moved up and hovered before the Jade Emperor.

"This is the pen of Author Wu," the Emperor said.

"Emperor," Confucius said, "pronounce your sentence. There's no reason to get excited over a flying pen."

The Emperor glared at Confucius. "Prime Minister, this just isn't any pen. The *chi* of a departed author is likely to reside most powerfully in exactly one place: *His pen.*"

Confucius looked as if he were about to pass out.

Nick wanted to applaud, but his hands were tied.

"What's going on?" Monkey whispered.

Beside him Kwan muttered, "Can it really be?"

The pen zipped past the court clerk and whisked a piece of paper up to the dais before the Dragon Throne. Then it began to write.

As it wrote, the Emperor read the words, but

for some reason Nick heard them in Author Wu's voice.

"Most High Emperor, please forgive this most unorthodox testimony. I hope you will understand that one who no longer exists has very limited options."

Confucius broke in. "Emperor, you can listen to this—"

The pen stopped writing, zipped down, and poked Confucius in the eye. The Prime Minister staggered backward and fell flat. It was all Nick could do to not burst into laughter. Monkey didn't have the restraint. Neither did many in the galleries. It seemed that seeing Confucius get some payback was a popular thing in Heaven.

Even the Emperor covered a laugh.

The pen zipped back up and continued writing, with the Emperor reading.

"Now, where was I? First, the Scholar From Above speaks the truth. Shu murdered me, after holding me prisoner against my will for five hundred years."

"That's a lie!" Shu shouted.

Confucius, who had managed to get back to his feet, waved a paper. "I have a sworn statement contradicting—"

Again the pen stopped writing and zoomed toward Confucius, this time poking a hundred holes in the document until it was nothing more than tatters. Then it zoomed back up and began writing again.

"Of course," the Emperor said, reading as the pen wrote, "I was brainwashed. But this human and the rest of these fine pilgrims finally opened my eyes to the value of my book, which I beg you to preserve for the sake of mankind in the world above, where it belongs."

Nick glanced over at Shu and the Masters. They were looking very, very panicked.

"Though these prisoners caused great havoc and damage in Heaven, they did so to right a wrong which had long festered in your kingdom. I defer to the Emperor's great wisdom and mercy."

The pen, with a flourish, finished by signing, "Wu Cheng-En."

At that point, the pen flew back to Nick and snuggled into his front pocket, where it stopped moving.

"Your highness," Shu shouted, "we must protest."

Confucius stared at the Emperor. "You can't possibly rely on the testimony of a pen," he said. "Only an idiot would—"

Suddenly Confucius realized what he had said.

The Emperor looked at his Prime Minister. "Are you dictating how we should rule?"

Confucius took a deep breath. "Confucius says never argue with an Emperor."

"Well then, Prime Minister," the Emperor said, his voice full and angry, "how did Author Wu die?"

Nick held his breath. This was the final moment of truth.

Confucius glanced at the Masters and Shu, then up at the Emperor. "Well, now that I think about it, there was so much commotion, I suppose it is possible Shu could have killed him."

The crowds broke into a roar.

Shu shouted, "Lies! Lies!"

It took a short time, but order was restored.

"Guards," the Jade Emperor ordered, "arrest the Seven Masters and untie the Human From Above, Monkey, and his friends."

Again pandemonium broke out in the massive hall. Confucius finally started banging his staff to bring order to the building.

As Shu was tied, he suddenly shouted at the Emperor, "Enemy of China! Immoralist! Your throne has lost the favor of Heaven. This court has no authority over me!"

"Take them out of here!" Confucius ordered.

Nick was shocked. "Wrong thing to say, Master Shu."

Shu just spit at him.

As the Varjipranis were tying up the Masters, Monkey shouted over, "Don't forget to use the Miraculous Tightening Knot. Mind if I demonstrate?"

"You flea-ridden ape!" Shu shouted back. "You think you defeated me? This is not the end!"

"Order!" Confucius shouted.

As the guards were leading the Masters out, Monkey jumped on the table and mooned them. Nick, Kwan, Pigsy, and even Friar applauded.

Nick turned to Friar. "Now *that* is funny."

Friar nodded and smiled.

"Now!" the Jade Emperor said after the Masters were gone. "Let us restore order."

A clerk took the barely visible copy of the original manuscript of *Journey to the West* and placed it in Nick's hands. It felt so light, so nonexistent, he tried not to move. The last thing he wanted to do was cause it any more damage.

Above them, the Emperor put his palms together and a powerful white light radiated from his forehead. It was so bright, Nick had to squeeze his eyes closed.

The book in his hands seemed to get heavier and heavier. Then the light faded and Nick held a fully restored manuscript.

"Now go, Scholar," the Emperor said. "Return the book to your world." Then he smiled. "And try not to cause any more trouble along the way."

Holding the book, Nick dropped to his knees. Everyone around him did the same as the Emperor left the building. Nick couldn't even find the words to say thank you.

Again Nick found himself back on the side of the mountain where he had rescued Monkey. The golden steps were there again, leading up to the gate into the real world. The sun was shining and the light seemed even brighter than before.

"It has been an honor to study with you, *Shih-Fu*," Friar said.

"I don't think I taught you much," Nick said.

"I did not learn to laugh," Friar said. "But

it was enjoyable to see how much laughter your actions inspired in others."

Nick looked at the Friar, not exactly sure how to take that. Finally he laughed and they saluted each other. "You're a funny guy," Nick said. "You know that?"

The next instant Pigsy hugged Nick, squeezing so tight Nick wanted to squeal. "I'm going to diet," Pigsy said. "Honest. I'll make you proud of me, Scholar."

Nick held Pigsy at arm's length. "To be honest with you, Pigsy, some people look better with a few extra pounds."

"They do?" Pigsy asked, his eyes bright.

"They do."

"Oh, now you've done it," Monkey said. "He'll eat everything he sees now."

Nick stepped in front of Monkey. "My teacher."

Monkey shook his head. "I'm not worthy of that title. I deserted you in your time of need."

"On the other hand," Nick said, "it looks as if you were right." Nick tipped his head in the direction of Kwan, who was standing a short distance away practicing her spells. Nothing was working. "I can't let her give up her powers."

"Until she regains her love for her work," Monkey said, "they will never return."

Nick nodded. "Then there is one last mission I have to complete." He moved toward the woman he loved more than anything else in the universe. As he stepped up beside her, she stopped her practice and smiled at him. The smile lit his heart, but he held the feeling back.

"Look, Goddess," he said. "I think that—"

"I've been thinking," she said, stopping him. "Maybe I could come up to your world with you. We could spend some time together. Have a few drinks. You could teach me how to look both ways before crossing the street."

His heart just about jumped out of his chest. She wanted to be with him, to live with him, but that would mean she would have no powers. She would lose everything she had worked for over centuries.

"I mean, if that's what you want," Kwan said.

He forced himself to look away from her eyes. He couldn't say what he had to say while looking at her. That was impossible. "Look, I don't think that's such a good idea."

She took a step back, his words clearly hurting. He wanted to reach out for her, hold her, tell her he was doing this for her own good, but he forced himself to remain still.

"I see." Her voice was cold and barely under control.

"I'm sorry," he said, forcing himself to go on, to break his own heart as well as hers. "I do love you, Goddess, for all the good that you do. But not—"

"But not as a woman."

He nodded, not trusting himself to say anything more.

"It's OK if I don't accompany you up the stairs to the gate?"

He nodded again.

With tears in her eyes, she turned and ran for the woods. The minute she vanished, he dropped to his knees and pounded the ground over and over with his fist. "Damn! Damn! Damn the Jade Emperor, damn all his creation! And damn me!"

Monkey, Friar, and Pigsy moved over and helped him to his feet.

"Scholar," Monkey said, "for once in my life, I was wrong. Human love can be selfless."

"Then why do I feel as if I have died and gone to hell?"

Nick pulled away and, with the book under his arm, he headed for the stairs as Monkey saluted him.

Twenty-two

Nick climbed the front stairs into the old building on the Xian University campus. Back when he was in college, he would have given anything to study in these buildings. Back before Linda.

Now he just wanted to drop off the manuscript and leave. Kwan had kept her promise, and only a day had passed in the real world. He could still make his meeting with Harding and the rest and put the last adventure into buried history. But he had to hurry.

Nick found the door labeled Professor Sheng and knocked.

"Come in," a voice said.

"I'm sorry, Professor Sheng," Nick told the man behind the cluttered desk. "You don't know me. My name is Nicholas Orton."

"Sorry for the mess." The old man motioned for Nick to come in.

"Not a problem," Nick said. "I can only stay a moment. I have something I'd like to donate to the university."

Nick tried to put the manuscript down on the

desk, but there was no room. Quickly Sheng made a space in the clutter.

Nick opened the cloth he had covering the manuscript and put the large book on the desk.

Sheng nodded. "It looks very old indeed. Where did you get it?"

"If I told you," Nick said, "you would never believe me."

"Journey to the West," Sheng said, reading the title. "Is this the Chu text?"

"No," Nick said. "It's the original."

"You mean the Yang version?" Sheng asked, becoming excited.

"This was written by the pen of Wu Cheng-En himself."

Sheng stared at the manuscript for a second, then leaned down and swept everything else off his desk, leaving only the manuscript in the center.

"But that's impossible," he said, bending over it.

"I assure you, it is not impossible."

As Sheng studied it, Nick could tell the professor started to believe it wasn't impossible as well.

"I must place a call immediately to the country's leading Monkey King scholar, Professor Chiao of Shanghai University. She must fly here at once to verify your claim of authenticity."

Nick nodded and stepped back toward the door as the professor moved to the phone. As he was dialing, Nick stepped out into the hall and ran for the front door of the building. With luck and a fast cab, he'd make the meeting right on time.

The cab got him to the Ministry of Communications just as Harding, Elizabeth, Benjamin, and Clark piled out of a limo. Nick thought he might feel excited to see them, but he felt nothing. He didn't like any of these people. This was just a job. He didn't have to like any of them.

"Sorry I'm late." Nick put on his best smile and joined them as they climbed the stairs into the building.

Harding glanced at him and frowned.

"Where have you been?" Clark asked. "I've been calling around for you."

"Just had to take care of a few details," Nick said.

The memory of Monkey, Pigsy, Friar, and Kwan came back strong. He wondered what they would think about what he was doing right now. More than likely they would laugh.

Inside, the meeting got started slowly, as Nick knew it would, and then kept going on and on, detail after detail. One side down the long wooden table wanted one thing, Harding's side wanted another.

Detail after deadly dull detail.

How could doing this ever compare with fighting demons and rescuing an entire world?

Nick tried to force himself to stay tuned in, but his mind kept wandering back to Kwan Ying.

Back to wondering what she was doing now.

Back to what he had said to her.

In his hand he held Author Wu's brush-pen, and as the meeting went on, he found himself scrawling Chinese characters on a sheet of blank paper.

Verse.

At one point Nick pushed the paper in front of one of the members of the opposite group. "Poetry," Nick whispered, when the man gave him a startled look. "You think it's any good?"

From down the long table, Harding gave him a cold look and kept talking.

Nick didn't care. He went back to writing with the Great Author's pen and thinking about Kwan and Monkey and the rest.

More verse.

More poetry.

It made a lot more sense than the stupid meeting.

In the Jade Palace dungeon, Shu and the Seven Masters were being held in magic-spelled cells, awaiting their trial. In front of them Confucius paced, his face red, his wounds not yet healed from his fall from the Gate.

"Don't you understand?" he said. "I've already done all I can for you."

"You betrayed us!" Shu shouted, his voice rocking the cells.

"I had no choice," Confucius shouted back, standing and facing the Master. "Your movement is dead. Try again in another five hundred years."

"No," Shu said, his voice low and mean. "I will not allow that to happen."

"You have no choice."

Shu stepped closer to the bars. "What do you think the Emperor would do if he found out his Prime Minister had been contravening his will all along? You sent his troops against the Monkey kingdom without his knowledge, for instance."

Confucius stopped and stared at Shu. "You wouldn't."

Shu smiled. "Master Shu says, *You scratch my back, I'll scratch yours.*"

Confucius shook his head in disgust. He knew when he was trapped.

Behind him in the cells, the Seven Masters started to laugh. It was a horrible sound.

Nick had long ago given up on trying to pay attention to the meeting. Instead, he spent the entire afternoon working on the poem. After a while, Harding and the others quit bothering him with stupid questions that really mattered to no one. What had become important to him was the poem.

And now, finally, he had finished it.

He jumped to his feet, put the brush in his pocket, and headed for the door.

"Where are you going?" Harding demanded.

"I finished the poem," Nick said. "I need a break. I'm pooped."

Harding looked more stunned than Nick could ever remember the man looking. Nick waved at him and turned toward the door. But then something outside the window caught his attention.

Black clouds, angry and boiling, were rushing toward the city over the horizon, from the direction of the gateway into the tomb.

"Mr. Orton!" Harding demanded. "What the hell are you up to? Now sit back down before—"

Nick bolted to the window. "No, it can't be." But he knew in his gut it was what he feared.

Rings of energy broke from the dark clouds and headed directly for the Ministry building.

"Under the desk!" Nick shouted. "Everyone! Now!"

For a second everyone froze. Then the tone in his voice and his command got people scrambling.

An instant later the roof exploded, sending wood and furniture flying everywhere. Only the long table remained in place.

Above Nick, the roof was gone.

"What happened?" Harding shouted.

"Stay back and down!" Nick ordered.

From out of the black clouds, seven figures materialized, their long robes billowing in the powerful winds.

Shu laughed, the sound echoing over the city like a doomsday toll. "The revolution has begun."

"Yeah, right," Nick said.

Shu dropped through the open roof to stand on the table. He looked around. "We should have thought of this eons ago. There's more than one way to stop a clock."

He fired an energy ring at the wall clock, exploding it.

Elizabeth screamed. Everyone else ducked for cover except Nick.

Outside, the other Masters were firing energy rings at buildings, water towers, cars, anything that looked modern. It was clear to Nick they planned on bringing down the entire city, and maybe the world, one detail at a time.

"We are your superiors." Shu said on the table with his hands on his hips in a Superman pose. He looked just plain stupid doing it, Nick thought. "We have come to restore traditional values to your world."

"Traditional values?" Harding stood up and stared at Shu. "You mean like 1950s values?"

"No, you idiot!" Shu yelled.

For an instant Nick was worried about Harding's life, but instead Shu went on talking.

"I mean traditional *traditions*. Those on which all civilization was founded. Before all of this was invented." One right after another Wu blew up lightbulbs, ballpoint pens, an electric teakettle, and a light pole outside the window.

"And before we knew people like you," he said to Harding, "even existed."

Shu laughed and then turned to Nick. "Where's your menagerie now?"

"Give it up, Shu," Nick said. "This place will be swarming with Heavenly Troops in no time."

An energy ring smashed into Nick and tossed him against the wall.

"Do not contradict your elders!" Shu shouted. Then, in a calmer voice, he went on. "Confucius has remade seven ordinary prisoners in our images. No one in Heaven will even know we're gone."

Harding looked at Nick as Nick climbed to his feet. "Orton, what is he talking about?"

Nick ignored Harding as Shu went on.

"And if that false Emperor ever finds out, we'll be ready for war, with humans as our front-line troops."

Shu walked along the top of the long wooden table toward Nick. "Now give me back my manuscript and we'll end all this progress very quickly."

Nick looked around the room, then winked at Harding. "Looks like I don't have it. Oops."

Shu fired another energy ring at Nick, again smashing him back into the wall. His breath was knocked out of him, but he couldn't let Shu know he was hurt. He pushed himself to his feet and stood there.

Before Shu could strike again, one of the other Masters landed beside him. "We have located the manuscript at the university."

Shu nodded. "Good." He turned to look at Harding and the others. "These barbarians are of no further use to the Revolution."

Nick felt Author Wu's brush-pen jumping in his pocket. He grabbed it and said, "Grow."

It became the weapon in his hands he had grown comfortable with.

Shu fired a deadly energy bolt at Harding and the others, but Nick stepped in the way and deflected it with his staff, then swiped his weapon through the air in a blur of motion.

"Run!" he shouted to Harding and the others.

Harding and the others stood riveted as Nick fought off one shot after another.

"I said get out!"

This time they moved.

Shu grew tired of the fight and lifted off into the air. Then he threw a massive energy ring at the building itself.

Nick felt the floor drop out from under him and the others, but he kept himself from being swallowed by spinning the brush as fast as he could.

Above him he heard Shu say to one of the other Masters, "We'll retrieve the manuscript, then come back for that human. I want to deal with him in person."

Nick lowered himself to the sidewalk as the Seven Masters moved off slowly, blowing up everything that offended them, which seemed like just about everything.

Nick dropped to his knees on the sidewalk. "Kwan Ying! Can you hear me? I need you now!"

He repeated his prayer three times without feeling her presence, then jumped up and hailed the nearest cab. He yanked the cabby from behind the wheel, made a quick apology, then drove off after the Seven Masters.

Somehow, he had to save the manuscript. And this time it looked as if he would have to do it alone.

Twenty-three

The Convent of the Bodhisattvas was carved out of the mountainside on the outskirts of the Jade Emperor's city. Beautiful towers thrust into the sky, supporting hanging gardens and a million flowers. A waterfall cascaded over the rocks beside it, and the view of the Jade City was spectacular.

One of the best views was from the high-ceilinged office of Mother Superior. But at the moment, neither Mother Superior nor her charge, Kwan Ying, were interested in the sights and beauty.

"Some of my powers have returned," Kwan said from her position on the couch in front of the Mother Superior's massive wooden desk, "though flying remains impossible."

Kwan was distracted. When her powers had started to return, the first thing she could do was spark beams of light from her fingers. Now she was shooting one colored beam after another, not really paying any attention.

"This human," Mother Superior said, "the Scholar. Are you still watching over him?"

"Oh, no," Kwan said. "As soon as he left, I

cut the karmic link between us. I didn't want to see or hear him any longer."

Mother Superior made a note on a pad, nodding. "But still your powers are slow to return. Interesting."

Kwan stopped playing with the light from her fingers and sat up straight. "Mother Superior, when I first lost my powers, it seemed like the most terrible thing in creation. Now, as they come back, they don't seem so miraculous anymore."

"I see," Mother Superior said. "Does anything?"

Kwan thought for a moment, then nodded. "Human beings. That they can come together without any powers at all and still make magic." Kwan smiled. "That's a miracle."

"It sounds as though you still love someone else more than you love your powers."

Kwan shook her head. "Then it is hopeless. As the humans say, it takes two. And he told me he doesn't love me."

Mother Superior smiled at Kwan, trying to be as gentle as she could be. "Dear Sister, it has been many incarnations since you were a human. But if you want once more to know their joys, you must also be willing to do as they do, and take a chance for the thing that you love."

Kwan nodded. "I know, but—"

Suddenly Nick's voice was there—faint, but there, echoing in her mind.

"Dear Buddha," Kwan said. "It can't be."

"What's wrong?"

"I think I hear him calling to me." Kwan

shook her head. "But that's not possible. I severed all links."

Kwan went into a trance and again connected the link with Nick. Suddenly she was seeing what he was seeing.

He was in a taxi, driving madly through the city as things collapsed around him from explosions. In the sky she could see figures.

The Seven Masters!

She stood. "I've got to help him. But how am I going to get to his world?" Her panic was as deep as it had ever been. She had to get to him, help him. She could not lose him now.

Inside she felt something shift and grow, as if a dam had let go that had been holding her energy back.

Slowly she rose into the air. But there was no cloud under her.

Kwan looked at the surprised Mother Superior. "What's going on? Where's my cloud?"

"It seems," Mother Superior said, "that you have found a new source of magic."

Nick had almost made it to the university when he saw the building where he had left the manuscript explode. He slid the cab to a stop and jumped out, his brush growing in his hands as he moved.

The dust was still settling around the building. Shu and the Masters were floating over the street. Only Professor Sheng was left standing in the rubble. In his hand was the manuscript.

"I will not allow you to harm this book!" Sheng shouted to the Masters.

Shu laughed and smashed Sheng aside, tossing him onto a mound of concrete.

Nick, using the brush to pole vault over the rubble, landed beside where the book had fallen.

"Stop now and the Jade Emperor may show you mercy."

Shu shook his head. "You're determined to die sooner rather than later, aren't you, human?"

While Shu remained above the action, the other Masters moved down and surrounded Nick.

"Reinforcements will be arriving in no time," Nick said, his brush moving as fast as it could go, guarding his back and sides.

"Really?" Shu asked. "And what makes you so certain?"

"I prayed to Kwan Ying."

The Skeleton Master moved toward him and Nick hit him, smashing him into a thousand bones.

"I think she loved me. Maybe she still does."

The Skeleton Master's bones reformed and he joined the others.

"Haven't you figured it out yet?" Shu laughed. "She's the Goddess of Mercy. She makes everyone think she loves them."

Two of the Masters moved at once, but Nick fought them off.

Then all of them moved, piling in on him like a football team tackling a quarterback. He took out a couple of them, but before he knew it he was imprisoned by floating Energy Rings.

Shu landed and picked up the manuscript. "I've waited five hundred years to put this world right."

Suddenly Kwan's voice came from out of the sky. "Did I hear aspersions cast on my good name a moment ago?"

Shu whirled around to see Kwan appear in the air. Nick was impressed. Her body literally glowed with power and energy.

By her side, Monkey, Pigsy, and Friar were in fighting stances.

"Why, Goddess and friends," Shu said. "What a surprise."

"You harm one hair on his head," Kwan said, indicating Nick, "and I will hunt you down through a hundred incarnations."

Nick smiled at her. She still cared.

"You've made your point," Shu said.

The Masters moved away and the Energy Rings around Nick vanished.

Kwan Ying floated down and stood in front of Shu. "Return the manuscript. We will escort you to face the Jade Emperor's judgment."

Smiling, Shu held out the book.

Nick knew instantly something was wrong. It was a trap.

"Goddess!" he shouted.

Too late.

She reached out to take the book, but instead Shu popped the lid off a tiny matter-nothingness urn. Two cloud-hands reached out and grabbed her.

Quickly Shu replaced the urn's lid and held it up for all to see. Kwan was trapped.

The Energy Rings again formed around Nick.

"Stand back," Shu said as Monkey, Friar, and Pigsy started to move at him. "Or I will order the dragons inside this to spit fire, subjecting her to unspeakable agony."

Monkey raised his cudgel, then stopped.

"Listen to me, fur-face," Shu said to Monkey. "For once, think before you act."

Shu backed away from Monkey and the others until he was standing near where Nick was imprisoned. Nick could see the jar holding the Goddess. Only the energy field separated him from the jar.

"Well." Shu smiled at Monkey. "It seems the balance of yin to yang has shifted once again. Your appearance complicates our plans, but fortunately, old traditions die hard."

Shu held up the urn holding the Goddess. "With our hostage in hand, we'll set up a new base in this world."

Nick stared at the urn. It would be so easy to dive through the energy rings and knock it from Shu.

Nick, don't do it!

Nick glanced around, then realized he had heard Kwan's voice inside his head.

The energy rings will kill you.

"What does Lord Buddha say?" Nick whispered, hoping she could hear him. "That after we die, what remains on Earth are the consequences of our actions."

Nick! No!

"Goddess, I love you," Nick said. "Now, and for all time."

With that, he dived through the energy rings. The pain was the worst he had ever felt. His skin burnt off his body, but he kept his entire focus on the urn.

And he hit it.

The last thing he remembered seeing was the urn flying through the air toward Monkey.

He had saved her. It was worth dying for.

Only death didn't last very long.

The next instant, he found himself standing, looking down at his own body as it faded away.

Monkey, Friar, and Pigsy were making short work of the Masters as they tried to run. Kwan was already out of the urn and bending over his quickly vanishing dead body.

She glanced up at where he was standing, then smiled at him and stood. "I suppose you'd like to know what's going on."

He looked at what was left of his burnt body, then nodded. "Yeah, that might be a good idea."

"I couldn't be certain whether or not this would happen," she said. "There's no way to judge the purity of another's actions."

"I'm still confused," Nick said. "Didn't I die there?"

"In a way, yes," she said. "Don't you remember in *Journey to the West*, what happened to the priest when he finally attained perfection?"

"He watched his old body die," Nick said,

staring at the faint outline of himself on the ground, "to be reborn into a state of enlightenment." He looked at her and her wonderful smile and loving eyes.

"Happy birthday, Nick."

He stepped forward and kissed her.

And she returned his kiss.

As they kissed, they floated off the ground, letting their bodies become one.

"Excuse me," a voice said from what seemed like a great distance away. Inside the link between them, Nick and Kwan both laughed.

"Oh, perfect beings?"

Nick and Kwan broke the kiss and looked around. The Seven Masters were leashed together with heavenly rope and Monkey, Pigsy, and Friar were smiling the biggest grins Nick had ever seen.

"What?" Nick said. "Can't a guy kiss his girl after he dies without everyone watching?"

"Sure thing, Scholar," Monkey said. "And there will be lots of time for that as soon as we deliver these Violators of Heaven to their Eternal Judgment."

"Right." Kwan straightened her hair. "Duty first."

A moment later they were all standing in the vast cavern that held the Terracotta Warriors. Only at the moment, the Warriors were all moving and very active. Nick could still remember the feeling he'd had when he was showing Harding and the others around. Now he felt a part of it. He felt as if he knew the Warriors.

And it seemed the Warriors were all happy to see him as well.

A few moments after they arrived, the Jade Emperor arrived with his entourage. Confucius, looking very nervous, was beside the Emperor.

It took Nick, Kwan, and Monkey very little time to explain what had happened and how it had happened.

The Jade Emperor did not look happy. "Supreme Lord Confucius, we have heard evidence that you aided the escape of these criminals and sought to conceal this fact from Heaven. Can you deny the charge?"

Confucius, looking down at the dirt on the chamber floor, said, "I cannot."

Shu spoke up. "We haven't even begun to tell you how he helped us attack the Monkey Kingdom with your troops."

Confucius bowed in front of the Emperor. "But, Your Highness, if I helped the Seven Masters, it was only in hopes of restoring the traditions of our great Chinese civilization to this world of humans."

"No!" the Emperor shouted. "You claim that such extreme beliefs serve Chinese values? This is an affront to our great history and culture."

Nick found himself nodding. Beside him, Kwan took his hand, listening as well to the words of a very wise Emperor.

"The goal of Chinese civilizations," the Emperor said, "has always been to find a Middle Way, far from the rigidity of extremes. Discipline and order play a part, yes, but only when

balanced by respect for creativity and the freedom of individuals."

The Emperor turned toward the trembling
Confucius. "Supreme Lord Confucius, you are
one pillar of our Heavenly Kingdom. But I have
no choice but to demote you to Protector of
the Heavenly Stables."

Confucius nearly passed out on the ground.
Monkey just laughed, as did many of the Warriors watching.

"As for the Seven Traditional Masters," the
Emperor said, turning to them, "you have vio-
lated the will of Heaven in open rebellion
against our authority. For your crimes—"

Suddenly the sound of chanting filled the
chamber. An intense light flooded the room.

Nick covered his eyes.

Then the light was gone.

Floating in a lotus position in the air in front
of all of them was what looked to Nick to be a
young monk. He was holding his hand in the
Buddhist sign of greeting.

"Xuanzang," Kwan whispered, clearly in awe
of the new arrival.

The minute she said the name, Nick knew it.

"I bring peace from the Buddha," Xuanzang
said.

"It is our old Master," Friar said.

"The Tang Priest," Nick said, stunned, "from
Journey to the West."

"Yes." Kwan squeezed his hand.

Monkey seemed just plain speechless.

"Sorry to interrupt," Xuanzang said. "I come
as emissary from the Jade Truth Monastery on

Holy Mountain, where serenity and inner contemplation are our primary concerns."

Xuanzang nodded to the Emperor, then turned to face Nick and the others. "The Lord Buddha himself has kept watch over these events, and he is pleased to reward my former companions for their diligence."

Nick looked around. They were all smiling, just happy to have been noticed.

"To Pigsy," Xuanzang said, "we award the rank of Buddha."

Nick thought Pigsy's face was literally going to light up enough to brighten the room. He tried to say thank you, but nothing came out.

"To our old friend Monkey, we bestow the coveted title of Teacher."

"Master," Monkey said, "I cannot accept such an honor."

Xuanzang glanced over at the Emperor. "He really has changed, hasn't he?"

The Emperor laughed.

"If anything," Monkey said, "the Scholar taught *me*, among other things, to respect the power of human love."

Nick squeezed Kwan's hand, and she returned the gesture.

"Foolish Monkey," Xuanzang said, "do you not understand that the mark of a true teacher is one who learns from his students?"

Now it was Monkey's turn to be speechless.

"As for Friar Sand, who has long sought the ability to laugh, this is not a gift Buddha can grant."

Friar tried to hide his disappointment, but Nick could see it.

"Everyone has always told me it was impossible," Friar said.

"But consider this," Xuanzang said. "Author Wu agreed to go to the world above only because you did not laugh at his story."

Friar looked at his old Master. "You mean it is good to be humorless? That it is not a terrible personal defect?" Friar shook his head, thinking about it. "All these centuries, I have been worried for nothing."

Suddenly Friar smiled, then started to chuckle. "Now *that's* funny."

Nick and everyone else could only laugh with Friar. It turned out the big priest had a very infectious laugh.

Xuanzang turned to Shu and the Masters, his face suddenly serious. "As for the Seven Traditional Masters, The Most Holy Buddha has determined that, for their crimes, they shall remain here, in the land of the humans."

Shu clearly didn't mind that idea at all. Nick and the rest, including the Jade Emperor, were not happy.

But Xuanzang was not finished. "You will all be immediately transformed into earthworms so that your souls may spend the next millennia reincarnating once more through the cycles of karma."

Shu and the others looked at each other, horrified, as a flash of light took them, leaving behind only eight earthworms wriggling at the feet of a Terracotta Warrior.

"Perfect," the Jade Emperor said, smiling. "Much better than what I had in mind for them."

Monkey clapped and Friar actually giggled.

Xuanzang raised his hand to depart. "Thus speaketh the holy Buddha."

In the background, the sound of chanting monks filled the massive chamber. Everyone but Nick and the Terracotta Warriors began to glow.

"You're all going?" Nick asked, looking around.

"Do not worry, Scholar," Xuanzang said, "about the destruction in your world. All will be restored by the Buddha's decree."

Nick nodded and looked at Kwan, who was also glowing.

"You're leaving?"

She smiled at him and nodded.

"But hold on," Nick said. "How long until I get a real date with you? Five, six incarnations?"

"Not so long, my love," Kwan said. "Not nearly so long."

Nick stared at her secretive smile. She was clearly not telling him something.

"But I thought we'd start out simple, with dinner and a movie. There's a new club in town, with a DJ who plays—"

The chanting stopped.

Everyone was gone.

The chamber was empty except for a few thousand stone warriors. Nick felt lonelier than he had ever felt in his life.

"All right, then," he said to the Warriors. "I'll wait."

* * *

The original manuscript of *Journey to the West* sat safely on Professor Sheng's desk as Nick knocked and then entered. The stuff that had been on the desk was now in a large pile in the corner.

"Oh, there you are." Sheng smiled at Nick. "I was beginning to think you were never coming back."

"I had some unfinished business to take care of."

Sheng smiled again. "So is your business now finished?"

"Oh, you might say that."

Nick felt Author Wu's brush pen in his pocket, then looked at Sheng's books and office. His dream had always been to study here, at this university. Maybe he could make it happen.

"Professor," Nick said, "I'd like to study Chinese poetry here at Xian University."

Sheng looked up from the manuscript at Nick, clearly surprised. "There are procedures for admittance, you understand."

"Of course," Nick said. "I'm willing to—"

Sheng held up his hand for Nick to stop. "On the other hand, if your gift proves authentic, I can hardly believe admissions would deny your request."

Smiling, Sheng shook Nick's hand. "Somehow, Mr. Orton, I suspect we will never be bored with you around."

Outside a car pulled up. Sheng pointed at the window. "At last, Professor Chiao."

"The Monkey King scholar?" Nick asked. "Chiao is known throughout the world."

"Come," Sheng said. "Let's go greet the Professor."

As Nick stepped out of the building, Professor Chiao came around her car. She was wearing a broad-brimmed hat and an attractive dress. Nick was stunned. He had never realized Professor Chiao was so young.

Sheng hurried down the steps and took her bag, then turned and walked toward the building and Nick, chatting with Chiao.

"Ah," Sheng said, as they reached the steps, "this is Mr. Orton, the American who brought us the manuscript."

The impact of her gaze almost knocked him back a step. It was the face of Kwan Ying.

"Pleasure to meet you, Mr. Orton," she said in Kwan's voice. "It is not every day some American appears from nowhere bearing gifts, like a Scholar From Above."

Nick could not believe his eyes. He blinked, but her face, her eyes, her look did not change.

"Goddess?" he said.

Chiao looked at him with a funny smile. "That's very flattering, Mr. Orton," she said, "but I'm afraid I'm just a simple scholar." She extended her hand. "Professor Chiao, from Shanghai University."

Nick took her hand, and the minute they touched she could not take her eyes from him.

"Have we met?" she asked after a moment.

He smiled, suddenly understanding what had happened. She had given up her life in Heaven to be with him on Earth.

"Maybe," he said, "in another life."

She nodded, still not looking away.

Finally Professor Sheng got them to move inside, where together they looked over the original manuscript.

Ten minutes later, as the two of them talked and started to get to know each other, Nick thought he heard an odd sound.

Outside the window, on a small cloud, three figures stood applauding. Monkey, Pigsy, and Friar.

As Professors Chiao and Sheng bent over the manuscript, Nick gave the three friends the thumbs-up sign.

They returned it, their smiles lighting up the sky.

Then, as Professor Chiao looked up, they vanished.

"Something wrong?" she asked.

"Nothing at all," he said. "Nothing at all."

Together they went back to work. He was shoulder to shoulder with the woman he loved, doing the job he loved. This *was* heaven—no matter what anyone said.